SNOW, ICE AND BULLETS

From the Bridge came the call: "Stand by to embark passengers. G.I. Joe and Action Man report to port-side gangway with gear."

Ernie bent down to pick up the third set of equipment which had been spread out. "Shan't need this then," he murmured. "I'll stow it below. Good luck you blokes."

He put out a hand to shake with Action Man . . . and the ship flew apart amidships as it slid over the top of the first of forty-five mines which had been sewn just below the surface.

The ship seemed to leave the water with the force of the explosion. The mountain of water that had been thrown up by the exploding mine descended in a smothering torrent that beat Action Man to his knees.

The ship tilted sideways at an alarmingly acute angle. Another explosion ravaged the interior of the vessel. Action Man caught a glimpse of G.I. Joe lying with his head through the guard rails, about to fall into the sea below. He threw himself full length and grabbed the American's ankle, hauling him back . . .

3 cde

Other ACTION MAN BOOKS

HOLD THE BRIDGE
THE TAKING OF MONTE CARRILLO
OPERATION SKY-DROP

All published by CORGI CAROUSEL BOOKS LTD.

SNOW, ICE AND BULLETS

MIKE BROGAN

CORGI CAROUSEL BOOKS LTD
A DIVISION OF TRANSWORLD PUBLISHERS LTD

SNOW, ICE AND BULLETS
A CORGI CAROUSEL BOOK 0 552 52074 8

Originally published in Great Britain by Aidan Ellis
Publishing Ltd.

PRINTING HISTORY
Aidan Ellis edition published 1977
Corgi Carousel edition published 1977

Carousel Books are published by
Transworld Publishers Ltd.,
Century House, 61–63 Uxbridge Road,
Ealing, London W5 5SA
Made and printed in Great Britain by
Cox & Wyman Ltd., London, Reading and Fakenham

CONTENTS

SNOW, ICE AND BULLETS

CHAPTER ONE

SPECIAL ASSIGNMENT!

"When did you last go on leave?" Ernie Perkins ducked as he asked the question and bullets from a machine-gun whined viciously above his head and knocked lumps off the brick wall behind him.

Lying beside Perkins, Action Man stared into the night trying to locate the muzzle-flashes of the gun that had them pinned down. "I dunno, Ernie. Seems like years. Every time I'm due to go I get detailed off on a Special Assignment." He had an American Browning Automatic Rifle lying on the rubble before him and he squinted down the sights as he thought he detected a movement. "Hey, Ernie, stick your nut up a bit. Let 'em get a look at you. I think I know where our friend with the machine-gun is."

"You stick your head up! Stone me, it's dangerous!" But Ernie obligingly raised his head above the level of the fallen bricks and immediately the machine-gun began firing again.

Action Man had been right in his location of

the enemy gunner. His B.A.R. was already sighted upon the machine-gun site and as the muzzle-flashes confirmed his opinion, he coolly squeezed the trigger. The gun-butt thudded against his shoulder as a stream of bullets came from the muzzle and he kept his finger on the trigger until all twenty rounds in the magazine had been fired.

He looked at Ernie and winked. "Got 'em!"

Ernie Perkins was a small man, but broad in the shoulder and had the nature of a terrier. He had tried to grow a beard once but someone had told him he looked like a gnome in the Snow White story, so he shaved it off. He wished he was taller and not so ugly; in fact, he secretly wished he looked like Action Man.

Action Man was a shade over six feet with an athlete's physique that was all sinew and muscle. He had a square jaw and a slow smile and blue eyes, but his eyes in anger assumed the shade of ice-chips, cold, ruthless. Action Man liked Ernie Perkins and had a great respect for the little man's dogged courage.

They were in the same Commando Unit on Special Assignment . . . a seaborne raid on the French coast. Their mission was to blow up petrol storage tanks just beyond the harbour of Bretville. An hour ago they had fixed the explosive charges to the tanks and were expecting the time-fuses to come into operation at any moment.

While Ernie and Action Man had worked

their way past the storage-tank defences to fix the charges, the rest of the small assault force had occupied the German garrison in the port. Action Man and Ernie should have joined up with them by now, fighting their way back to the assault boats lying on the darkened beaches not eight hundred metres away but the Germans had quickly brought in reinforcements and they had found themselves cut off. They had moved to higher ground above the port, sheltering in an abandoned farm cottage.

There was no more firing from the machine-gunner and when Action Man raised his head above cover there was no answering burst of fire.

"You got 'em okay, Action Man," agreed Ernie admiringly. He nodded at the B.A.R. into which the big Commando had slammed a new magazine. "Where'd you get that?"

"G.I. Joe gave it to me. He reckoned he'd find a Sten handier in the street fighting down there." Action Man inclined his head at the shadowy outline of the port spread out below them. "So we did a swop." He hefted the American automatic weapon in his hands. "It's a great gun, too. I like it."

"Did for that lot all right." Ernie gestured forward at the darkness. "You'd have had to get a bit nearer to make sure with a Sten." He pushed his tin-hat back from his forehead and mopped his brow. "Wish those tanks would go up. Don't reckon the Jerries found the bombs do you?"

Action Man shrugged his shoulders in the half-light and was about to say he didn't know . . . when the bombs they'd planted on the storage tanks began to explode. The first dull thudding detonation was followed immediately by a blinding flash of light. Flames leaped a hundred feet into the air, illuminating more fat round tanks alongside. Then came further explosions at regular intervals and each one was followed by a fire-flash.

Roaring flames from the devastated petrol tanks reflected from the low-lying clouds above until it seemed as though the very sky itself was alight. The buildings and port installations came into bright relief as though it were daylight and in front of the ruined cottage where Action Man and Ernie Perkins were crouched they could see a long rutted track ran all the way downhill to the town.

Perkins grinned. His face was streaked with smoke and grime. "Looks like we got the jackpot," he said in satisfaction. "I'd call that . . . mission accomplished, wouldn't you?"

Action Man agreed. "All we gotta do now . . . is get back to our buddies and the boats. That could be difficult."

It was difficult. At first they saw no one as they moved cautiously down the rutted track. But then the track became a road with a proper surface and three hundred metres from the seafront twenty or thirty German infantrymen were under cover at the roadside, firing at the remainder of the Commando force who were dropping back to the beach. On the beach, ramp doors invitingly open, were three Tank Landing Craft.

The assault force had come ashore from the craft in jeeps, driving straight from the beach into the town. Most of the jeeps had been knocked out ashore but several of them had made the return journey safely.

From the Oerlikon guns on the bridges of the landing craft, the naval gunners were keeping up a steady fire, covering the withdrawal.

"All we have to do is get past that lot," said Ernie Perkins without much enthusiasm. "And we better do it smartly 'cos those boats ain't going to hang about too long. It's getting hot down there."

Most of the men of the assault force had reached the beach and as some of their number returned the German fire, other groups made dashes for the ramp doors. The raging inferno of the burning oil-storage tanks lit the scene as vividly as a play upon a theatre stage.

At the top of the road stood a group of three houses, and Action Man pointed the muzzle of his B.A.R. at them. "Reckon any of those houses have cars in their garages, Ernie? A car would be handy."

"Let's go and ask," muttered the little man. "Anyone living there ain't going to be asleep, not with this row going on. What do we want a car for, anyway?"

"Quickest way through that lot and down to the beach." Action Man was moving quickly towards the houses as he spoke. "Let's hope they're good French citizens . . . and not Jerries in there."

A middle-aged woman opened the door of the first house when they hammered on the door. She couldn't speak English well but could understand enough to know what they wanted. "M'sieur Aisles has a car. The house at the far end." She was frightened and as soon as they turned she banged the door behind them.

M'sieur Aisles was a stout, red-faced man with a spikey moustache. He was not happy to lend his car to Action Man and Ernie but agreed to do so. He led them reluctantly to a large shed at the far side of the house. The banging of machine-guns and the sharper crackling sound of rifle-fire served to hurry the man along.

"There!" he said, opening the shed door and gesturing inside. "There is not much petrol, half a gallon. Maybe it will start, maybe not. I have not used it for many months."

"The British Government will pay if it gets damaged," said Action Man, "I promise."

"When the war is ended, I suppose." The Frenchman shrugged his shoulders and spread his arms wide. "And if the British should win, too! Ah, well, take the car . . . I wish you bon chance, mes amis!"

The vehicle was an old Citroen saloon and to the surprise of the two Commandos, it started at the first attempt.

They backed out of the shed into the road. The Frenchman had vanished inside his house and all three houses were dark and silent apart from the flickering glow of the petrol fires reflected in the windows.

"Knock out the windows, we don't want a lot of glass flying around in here." Action Man used the butt of his B.A.R. to smash the windscreen while Ernie prodded out the side windows with his Sten-gun. "You take right-hand side and front . . . I'll take left-hand-side and front." Action Man slid the muzzle of the B.A.R. through the shattered windscreen and held on to it with one hand. With his other hand he engaged gear and the car moved forward.

The Germans shooting at the retreating assault force failed to hear the car coming down the road behind them until it was no more than twenty metres away and travelling fast.

A sergeant leaped to his feet, swinging a machine-pistol up and round. "Achtung! Achtung!" He managed the warning shout just before Action Man fired a short burst, knocking him backwards. The other Germans turned to bring their weapons to bear upon the rushing Citroen.

Bullets began to smack into the sides of the car. One hit a front tyre and Action Man pulled hard on the wheel to prevent the vehicle slewing

sideways off the road.

Ernie Perkins was firing steadily from the side window. As the car bucketed through the German line he transferred his attention to the back window, firing rapidly at the Germans now behind them.

"Use the B.A.R., Ernie," yelled Action Man. "Longer range. I can't use it. Got to steer now. Not so easy with a tyre shot out."

Two of the three landing craft had raised their ramp doors and were going astern away from the beach, swinging round to face the open sea. The third had started to raise its ramp door but the Captain must have seen the car hurtling down the road for the ramp suddenly banged down on the beach again. Above the noise of the gunfire, Action Man heard the sound of cheering. A dozen Commandos, safely aboard the craft were standing in the well-deck just beyond the ramp. They were waving their helmets and shouting encouragement. One of them stood on the ramp arms up like a policeman directing traffic, waving them aboard.

There were more Germans firing at them now. Infantry groups had moved up the beach on both sides and the Citroen drove into a murderous cross-fire.

They reached the end of the road and went on straight across the promenade. Beyond was a three metre drop to the beach and then ten metres of sand to the sea's edge.

Action Man's hands gripped the wheel until

the knuckles showed white and the muscles on his forearms stood out like whipcord. Bullets were slicing through the car and the dashboard suddenly disintegrated before him.

"Get down Ernie and hold tight. This is going to be rough."

Ernie Perkins turned to look forward just as the Citroen flew out off the promenade and took the three metre drop on to the sand. They landed with a crash that sent them lurching out of their seats, their heads smacking into the roof. But the car kept going forward. The doors burst open, the bonnet rose, blocking off Action Man's view and the boot door came up behind.

Action Man felt the car veer off course in the loose sand, turning against the drag of the wheel with the burst tyre. The driver's door had remained shut and he poked his head out of the window, peering around the impeding bonnet. The landing craft was six metres away and dead ahead.

Bullets were hitting the car regularly but the raised boot and bonnet were giving them cover. The front wheels juddered as they hit the ramp door of the landing craft and then they were inside.

"Brakes!" screamed someone.

Action Man took his foot off the accelerator which he had kept down to the floorboards and transferred it to the brake pedal. There was a screech as the tyres bit on the metal deck and then a tremendous crash and they came to rest.

Ernie Perkins climbed out rubbing his bruises and went to the front of the Citroen. It was embedded in the radiator of a jeep. Both machines were totally wrecked.

"That is going to cost the British Government quite a packet . . . if we win the war!" Ernie Perkins stood with his hands on his hips and a wide grin on his face. He seemed pleased.

Action Man inspected the damage, too. A voice from above called: "Welcome aboard, gentlemen!" He looked up and saw the blue peaked cap of a Naval Lieutenant, the face beneath smiled pleasantly. "You cut it a bit fine, I must say."

Action Man saluted. "Good to be aboard, sir." Beneath his feet the deck of the landing-craft began to rise and fall evenly as it met the swell of the Channel. "Thanks for waiting for us."

The other Commandos gathered around them clapping them on the back and laughing. "Reckon you two wouldn't get left," roared one of them. "Best couple of escape artists in the outfit."

Action Man had been looking at the faces around him. "Anyone seen G.I. Joe?" he asked. "Did he get off, too?"

"He's on one of the other craft. Had to tie him down almost. Wanted to go back ashore and find you. Grumbling something about you losing his gun."

Action Man leaned into the wrecked Citroen

and lifted out the B.A.R. "He ought to know better than that." He grinned. "Used all the ammo, though. Hope that won't upset him."

* * * * *

The following evening they were in the Commando barracks just outside Portsmouth. G.I. Joe was there waiting when Action Man and Ernie Perkins, still covered with the grime of battle, came into the big drill-hall where the other Commandos were stripping off their battle-packs.

He came towards them smiling, holding out his hand. "By hookey, am I glad to see you!" Ernie and Action Man extended their hands . . . and the American walked past them and picked up the B.A.R. leaning against the wall. He examined it fondly. "Boy, am I relieved to have you back. Best little gun in the business."

The big British Commando tapped G.I. Joe on the shoulder. G.I. Joe was as tall as Action Man with the same air of ready-for-anything about him. He had broad shoulders and an easy grin, but like Action Man, his eyes could quickly turn from warmth to the coldness of chilled-steel. Action Man tapped his shoulder again. "And what about me and Ernie Perkins? Aren't you glad to see us back, too? We had quite a job making it."

"Ahhh, you two! Who would worry about

21

you?" He winked at Action Man. "You and me have been in too many fights, buddy. No one ain't gonna worry about you. But this!" And he raised the B.A.R. "I worried about this."

"What for," asked Ernie. "Why you so worried?"

The American patted Ernie's cheek. "Cos it ain't mine, buddy-boy, that's why! I borrowed it . . . without asking, if you know what I mean. Its owner would be upset to find it gone missing."

"You nicked it," grunted Ernie, "that's what you mean."

"And you've got a nasty suspicious little brain," returned the American. He produced a Sten-gun and passed it to Action Man. "See. I looked after your gun. Reliable G.I. Joe, they call me."

"What do you reckon on us getting some leave?" said Ernie. "We did a good job over there, blowing up all those petrol things. I reckon we've earned some."

"Let you into a secret." The American grabbed both of them by their arms. "I heard it in the officers' mess. We're all going to get leave. Fourteen days. What about that?"

Colonel Cartwright, the Officer Commanding the Commando Barracks entered the drill-hall and every man there sprang to attention. "He's going to tell us about our leave," whispered G.I. Joe.

Cartwright made a short speech congratulat-

ing the men on the success of their raid and
ended by saying: "And now I'll tell you what
you've all been hoping to hear. Leave has been
arranged. Fourteen days."

There was a burst of cheering and the Colonel
had to raise his voice to make himself heard.
"As soon as you've cleaned up I want Action
Man, G.I. Joe and Private Ernest Perkins in my
office. Okay, men, carry on."

"What's he want us for?" Ernie Perkins'
voice was full of suspicion.

"Gonna give you a medal," suggested G.I.
Joe.

"G'arn, I don't believe it." Perkins made a
face. "We're gonna get our leave stopped for
something. I can feel it."

*   *   *   *   *

Colonel Cartwright's office was warmed by a
glowing stove and Ernie moved himself
appreciatively toward it. Action Man and G.I.
Joe lined up beside him facing the Colonel and
another man who sat watching them, his face
expressionless.

"At ease, men." Colonel Cartwright
indicated the civilian at his side. "This is Mr.
Blandment, from Army Intelligence, he's come
from London to see you three. He has a job for
you."

Action Man raised an eye-brow and glanced
sideways at Ernie Perkins as he whispered: "A

Special Assignment."

"What about our leave, sir?" asked Ernie Perkins. "This assignment. Will we get our leave before . . . or after?"

"After." The colonel's voice was crisp. "Action Man and G.I. Joe have been on these special duties before, of course. You, Perkins, are included as a reserve . . . what our American friends call a 'back-up' man." He glanced at G.I. Joe. "Is that the right term?"

"I guess so, sir," murmured G.I. Joe.

Cartwright looked at the man from Army Intelligence. "Perhaps you'd like to talk to them, sir?"

Mr. Blandment was tall and his face was angular and hawk-like. Black, bushy eyebrows gave him a forbidding expression. He said: "There's not much I can tell you now, except that you will all be flown up to Scotland immediately. There's no need to pack. You will be re-equipped at your destination. The job you are to carry out is one of great urgency and secrecy. You will tell no-one of this interview." He glanced at Colonel Cartwright. "I don't think it's necessary for me to say more at this stage and our plane is waiting for us."

A thin smile crossed his lips and he added: "I'm sorry about having to cancel your leave but you are the three best men for the work I have in mind. Perhaps . . . the only men who could bring it off. Shall we go?"

Colonel Cartwright wished them luck and

they left the barracks in a closed car. Twenty minutes later they were aboard a Dakota aircraft, heading north.

*   *   *   *   *

The next three weeks were ones of intensive training. They were billeted in a makeshift camp of wooden sheds in the Scottish Cairngorm mountains. The winter snow lay thickly upon the slopes and all three of them spent several hours a day on skis.

G.I. Joe and Action Man were expert skiers and they were surprised to discover that Ernie Perkins was almost as good as they were.

"Did a lot of it as a kid," he told them. "In Austria before the war. My dad was an engineer working over there and me and my mum used to spend holidays with him. All the Austrian kids could ski and I picked it up easily. Used to enjoy it, too."

"Must be why we three were picked for this job," said G.I. Joe. "I reckon we're probably the three best men on skis they could find."

And so it proved. During the three weeks, when they were not brushing up on their mountain skills, they were instructed in Norwegian geography; they learned a smattering of the Norwegian language; and they spent many hours getting in and out of a rubber dinghy and paddling it across one of the Scottish lochs. It was dull work but it made them very proficient.

They had not seen much of the man from Army Intelligence but one evening he came to their quarters and explained their mission.

"Briefly, this is what you will do," he said, settling himself on the corner of a table. "You will go aboard a coaster which will take you to the Norwegian coast by nightfall. You will leave the coaster by rubber dinghy and go ashore. A Professor Lindfors will be waiting in a house in a village and you will contact him and bring him back to England. That, basically, is your mission."

There was silence in the hut. The wind outside whistled eerily.

"Now to the details. Professor Lindfors was trapped in Norway when the Germans overran the country. He's a scientist and he has continued to work. His work is secret, of a military nature. The Germans want to use the professor's knowledge for their own ends but Lindfors prefers to give his knowledge to the Allies and he has been in touch with us and asked to be rescued. We have promised him we will bring him to England."

"Where's Lindfors now, sir?" asked Action Man.

"In a village called Voorsgaard not far from the coast where you will land . . . some thirty kilometres distant. When you bring the professor back, the coaster will be lying off-shore ready to pick you up."

"And we will have to use skis to get from the

landing place to Voorsgaard?"

"Yes. Fortunately the professor can ski almost as well as he can walk. There'll be no difficulty there."

"What about me, sir? You said I was a 'back-up' man. What do I have to do?"

"You go with Action Man and G.I. Joe as far as the Norwegian coast but you will stay aboard the coaster. You will only go ashore if either Action Man or G.I. Joe falls sick, or is injured. If that happens, you will take the ailing man's place."

G.I. Joe had been looking thoughtful for some time and now he said: "This Professor Lindfors, sir. He didn't used to be a college professor in America, did he? Before the War?"

"That's the man. And that is another reason why you were chosen for this mission. Professor Karl Lindfors taught chemistry in the college you attended, Joe. You know him. You will recognise him when you see him. It's important we don't bring out the wrong man."

"What if G.I. Joe goes sick and I have to take his place?" put in Ernie Perkins quickly. "Me and Action Man don't know him."

"You'll be shown photographs of the man. In the event of G.I. Joe dropping out we'll have to rely upon the photographs for identification . . . but we'd rather he was recognised by someone who knows him personally. It's safer." He sighed. "It would not be beyond the Germans to try a ruse such as substituting someone else in Lindfors' place . . . especially if they are aware that an attempt to rescue the professor is about to take place. Now, are there any more questions?"

No one spoke. The silence lasted a full minute.

Then the Intelligence man stood up and glanced at his watch. "Gentlemen, we'd better be moving. The coaster that takes you to Norway is waiting. You sail at once."

*   *   *   *   *

At half-past two in the intermittent light of a moon that appeared fleetingly from time to time from behind dark clouds, the high rocky cliffs of the Norwegian coast appeared ahead.

The ship Action Man and his pals were aboard nosed in closer through the ice-cold waters. There were icicles on the rigging and wire stays, and all metal objects on the exposed decks were dangerous to touch, so cold were they.

G.I. Joe, Action Man and Ernie Perkins were dressed in their Arctic survival kit, the fur-trimmed hoods of their anoraks raised around their heads. They stood in a group at the base of the ladder leading up to the bridge where two Royal Navy officers watched the shoreline slowly slipping by. They watched through binoculars, searching for the landmark that would tell them they had arrived at the place to launch the rubber dinghy in which two men would go ashore.

Ernie Perkins rubbed his gloved hands together and shivered. "Can't say as how I'm sorry to be staying aboard, mates," he muttered. "It's cold enough out here to freeze the flame on a match."

"Maybe you will go," grinned G.I. Joe, turning his steely eyes on Ernie. "I think I've got a broken leg."

"You mean you can't go and . . ." Ernie broke off as he realised the American was joking. "Oh, shut up, Yank. Stop messing about."

A voice above them called softly: "Stand by, chaps. We expect to be dropping you off in twenty minutes. Better check your gear once more. Make sure that rubber dinghy is okay. If that springs a leak and you go in the water . . . you'll find it extremely chilly."

The ship's engines which had registered a steady note of power in the background ever since they'd stepped aboard, died away and they felt the forward thrust through the water slacken slightly.

On the after deck, G.I. Joe and Action Man ticked off their equipment from a list they'd been given. Each man had a pair of skis, ski-poles, and a bulging pack which contained rations, torches, spare clothing, compass and maps. Beside each pack was propped a Sten gun with a long sling attached and with each gun was a neat stack of spare magazines.

Ernie had three sets of webbing equipment and he deftly inserted the spare magazines into the pouches while the other two men inspected the rubber dinghy which was lashed against the rails. It had been inflated two hours earlier and was still hard and compact.

Looking forward they could see the outline of two Oerlikon guns each side of the bridge. The gun crews were closed up and even as they watched they noticed both guns were slowly rotating, covering the dark clouds above.

A naval officer in a duffle coat came toward them.

"Expecting trouble, chum?" questioned G.I. Joe, nodding at the guns on the bridge. "Air raid or something?"

"Not much chance of that. Too much cloud," responded the Naval man confidently. "Just routine action stations," he explained. "We're well inside enemy waters. Don't want to be caught napping." He glanced at his wristwatch. "We've located your landing place. We'll be dropping you off in ten minutes. I just came aft to find out if you were ready."

"Ready and willing," grinned Action Man. "Sooner we get moving the better. Will you be the chaps who'll pick us up?"

The officer nodded. "We'll be lying off the coast every night now for the next week at this time. Flash the Morse letters POD and we'll send a boat in for you."

"POD?"

"Professor on delivery," came the answer with a grin. "Our skipper's got a sense of humour."

The ship had turned slightly inshore and the towering black cliff flecked here and there with snow and ice appeared very near.

From the bridge came the muted call: "Standby to embark passengers. G.I. Joe and Action Man report to port side gangway with gear."

Ernie bent down to pick up the third set of equipment which had been spread out. "Shan't need this then," he murmured. "I'll stow it below. Good luck you blokes."

He put out a hand to shake with Action Man . . . and the ship blew apart amidships as it slid over the top of the first of forty-five mines which had been sown just below the surface.

The ship seemed to leave the water with the force of the explosion. A great column of flame leaped out through the deck forward of the bridge and Action Man saw the bridge itself crumple slowly and totter sideways. Then the mountain of water that had been thrown up by the exploding mine descended in a smothering torrent that beat him to his knees.

In the same instant the ship tilted sideways at an alarmingly acute angle and everything loose rolled and jolted toward the dipping guard rails.

Another explosion ravaged the interior of the vessel as the already shattered hulk hit the second mine in the line. Action Man caught a glimpse of G.I. Joe lying with his head through the guard rails, about to fall into the sea below. He threw himself full length and grabbed the American's ankle, hauling him back.

G.I. Joe was dazed but unhurt.

"We've hit a mine. Two of 'em," yelled Action Man. "The ship's sinking!" And to confirm his words the coaster settled suddenly lower into the dark water.

"What's the skipper doing?"

Action Man shook his head. "The bridge went when the first mine went off. We don't have a skipper any more."

A further shudder shook the ship from stem to stern. The bows dipped and went under and G.I. Joe and Action Man began to slide down the steeply sloping deck. They both grabbed at a hatch cover and held on.

"The crew? Where are they?"

"I don't know." Action Man steadied himself and rose to his feet. "I don't see anyone. That officer we were talking to . . . he just vanished. Blown over the side, I think."

The bows dipped further and the stern rose clear of the water.

"Where's the rubber dinghy?"

"Gone."

"Reckon we'd better be gone, too. This tub's going to the bottom."

They struggled to the side. With the bows under water and the stern raised high, the water looked a long way below them.

"It's gonna be cold."

"It's our only way out. Stay here . . . and we'll go down with it."

"Little Ernie?"

"No sign of him. Come on, Joe . . . let's jump. I reckon we've got two minutes left. She's going!"

They both had one leg over the guard rails and were taking deep breaths before jumping when they heard a voice. It said: "Okay, jump. I've got you."

"What the heck?" G.I. Joe turned to look behind him.

"Down here," came the same voice. It was Ernie Perkins.

They peered down. Floating on the swell amid a growing mass of debris that floated out of the doomed ship was their inflated rubber dinghy. Sitting securely in the centre of it, Ernie Perkins. He had a paddle in one hand and waved at them with the other.

"For Pete's sake jump, you twits," the little man yelled hoarsely. "I've been paddling around looking for you two! If you don't get off that thing . . . you're going to the bottom with it."

The ship lurched terrifyingly and G.I. Joe and Action Man hesitated no longer. They pushed themselves clear and dropped.

The water was liquid ice. It beat the breath from their bodies. It squeezed their lungs in a vice-like grip. It felt as though it were crushing their skulls.

They surfaced, mouths gaping for air and both would assuredly have gone under a second time if Ernie Perkins, leaning perilously over the side of the rubber dinghy had not grabbed their collars and held them.

That brief second of respite enabled them to catch their breath; enabled them to gather their numbed senses; to realise that if they did not get out of the freezing water very quickly, they would die.

They both turned and grabbed the dinghy. Its fat swollen sides didn't help them, but they scrambled and strained and with Ernie tugging at them, managed to spill themselves over the edge . . . and to safety.

A paddle hit Action Man on the side of the face.

"Get moving, Action Man. Move." Ernie Perkins was yelling frantically. "Get that paddle and row, mate. It'll warm you up . . . and it'll get us away from that!"

Action Man stirred himself. The ice-cold water had numbed his senses completely, but he was recovering. Above him he saw the towering menace of the sinking ship. They had drifted in close under the stern and immediately above them were the knife-edged screws of the twin propellers. Both of them were still turning, revolving like the blades of a threshing machine.

But the dinghy was moving away. G.I. Joe had a paddle and was flailing away at the water.

Ernie too was working as hard as he could go and when Action Man joined in, the rubber boat slid away from the black menace of the hull. And just in time.

They were no more than forty feet away when the stern rose even higher above them and then, with a screeching noise that rose on the night air like the wail of a banshee, slid downward.

Within seconds the ship had vanished. Huge air bubbles rose on the surface and burst. Boxes, planks, chairs, tables, everything moveable within the ship that was not trapped came floating to the surface and spread in a sinister stain of death.

As though impelled by the same thought, they paddled toward the now gently rocking debris. To and fro they went, calling, but hearing no answering voice.

After a long time had passed, G.I. Joe stopped paddling and said, "If there was anyone . . . they'd be frozen stiff by now."

"No survivors. No one."

"Except us three." Ernie and G.I. Joe turned their heads to look at Action Man. He sat in the stern, a paddle across his knees, his eyes bleak.

"What do we do?" asked Ernie. "It's a long way home from here."

"We don't go home." Action Man nodded in the direction of the black cliffs. "We go thataway!"

"Ashore?"

"We'll be shoved in a POW camp."

"Why should we be? Why should we be captured at all?" Action Man's fierce words held the other two riveted. "Why don't we go ashore as we were going to . . . and carry on with our job?" He motioned across the debris-strewn waters, his lips a tight line. "I reckon those lads would rather we did that . . . they wouldn't have wanted to bring us out here . . . for nothing."

G.I. Joe nodded. "Okay, I'll go along with that. What about you, Ernie?"

"Me? I'll do what you fellers do," sniffed the little man. He rummaged around in the bottom of the dinghy and lifted out a pair of skis. "I wouldn't mind having a go in some real mountains . . . like those over there."

"Where the heck did you get those?" G.I. Joe stared at Ernie Perkins in bewilderment. "The skis, I mean."

"Fished 'em out the water, didn't I?" the little man groped further in the hidden recesses of the rubber boat. "When that mine went off, I was blown straight over the side, mate. An' everything went over with me. All our gear. I got most of it before it sank. The skis . . . the packs . . . most of the stuff. All except the guns, of course, they went down like stones." He sounded apologetic.

"Okay, let's go then." Action Man plunged his paddle into the water and the others did the same. They were feeling cold again. The exercise would warm them.

The dinghy began to move quickly across the surface. In the sky came the first hint of dawn's light . . . and the towering black cliffs looked higher than ever. As they drew closer into their shadow . . . they wondered how they would ever climb them.

CHAPTER TWO

WHERE'S THE PROFESSOR?

There was no beach or foreshore; the cold black rocks of the cliff dropped straight into the mirror-surface of the sea. They stopped paddling and allowed the dinghy to drift forward silently. All three looked upwards.

G.I. Joe was the first to put into words what the others were thinking: "That is one cliff that ain't climbable," he observed. "Look at it. No footholds, no hand-holds, nothin'! An' no beach to work from. Take it from me, buddies . . . if we're going ashore . . . it ain't gonna be here."

Action Man agreed with G.I. Joe but he didn't want to give up too easily and he paddled the dinghy nearer and nearer until they all reached out to fend off the towering black wall.

"We'll paddle along the foot of the cliff. There's got to be a break in it somewhere. A fissure of some sort. Something we can climb."

Paddling and hauling themselves along against the cliff-face they had covered several hundred yards when Action Man put up a hand to stay them. "Listen!" he whispered. "Engines!"

They stopped, hanging on to the cliff, motionless in a huge pool of dark shadow. They could all hear the noise now. The steady throbbing bom-bom engine noise of a boat.

"Sounds like something small," murmured Perkins with relief in his voice. "Fishing boat or something."

They waited. The sound came closer. And then quite suddenly they saw the silhouette of a short stubby hull and the stunted shape of a wheel-house set amidships. A small curve of white water foamed at the bows. Above the steady engine noise they could hear voices and the occasional flash of light as though someone were smoking a cigarette on the deck.

"Norwegian!" said Action Man. "You're right, Perky . . . it's a fishing boat."

They watched silently as the vessel moved steadily past them. It was almost out of sight in the half-light when it turned in toward the cliff and disappeared from view.

"Blimey, where'd it go?" Perkins looked from one to the other in astonishment. "It rammed the cliff."

G.I. Joe and Action Man picked up their paddles and G.I. Joe tossed the other to Perkins. "Get weaving, man, we're moving."

"We're following that boat," explained Action Man. "It's not rammed the cliff, Perky, old sport . . . it's turned into a creek or inlet.

And what's going to be at the other end?"

"Don't ask me, I've never been here before."
Perkins plyed his paddle with a will and the
rubber dinghy skimmed over the glass-like surface.

"A harbour," supplied G.I. Joe. "Why else
would a fishing boat turn up an inlet in the cliff,
eh?"

"Makes sense," Perkins agreed. He grinned.
"Glad we don't have to mess about trying to
climb that." He nodded at the towering cliff
walls. They had turned the corner now, following the fishing boat and the cliff rose high on
both sides of the inlet, enclosing them.

The dinghy began to rise and fall un-
comfortably, pitching and tossing on a giant
swell that came rippling towards them out of the
darkness.

"The wake of the fishing boat," said G.I. Joe.
"We can't be all that far behind it."

"Keep paddling, they can't see us, even if
they were looking for us," Action Man declared. "The closer we get the better. Some of
these fjords twist and turn and widen out. We
don't want to get lost."

They bent to the paddles again, moving
swiftly, riding the recurring mounds of the fishing boat's wake. Near at hand, against the base
of the cliff, they could hear the slap-slap of the
water striking the rocks.

Half an hour passed. All three of them were
tiring rapidly when, in the half-light, they

rounded a buttress of the cliff and saw the fishing boat, moving slowly, less than a hundred yards ahead. And beyond, a stubby quay. Beyond again were a collection of gable-fronted wooden houses and long sheds. The houses formed a neat pattern against the towering mountains rising behind.

"What now?" Ernie Perkins looked from Action Man to G.I. Joe. "If we hang about, it'll be daylight and someone's going to spot us."

"We'll go ashore." Action Man pointed to the extreme right-hand edge of the fishing community before them. "Over there where the houses end."

Five minutes later they were wading towards land through a jumbled mass of jagged rocks, carrying the stuff from the dinghy that Ernie Perkins had managed to salvage. It was still not quite daylight.

When their packs and skis were ashore, Action Man gestured to the others to return to the dinghy. "Sink it," he ordered. "If the Germans find it they'll start searching for whoever landed here . . . us!"

They heaped the interior of the boat with rocks and then slashed the rubber hull below the water line. Within seconds their method of arrival had disappeared below the surface.

"Somewhere to hide and somewhere to dry out and eat, that's what we want now." The big British Commando grinned at his companions. "Anyone got a better idea?"

The other two shook their heads and Action Man nodded to G.I. Joe. "You go and find a place. An empty shed, something like that. If you're not back in half an hour, we'll move on . . . assuming you've found trouble." His eyes were bleak as he added: "Remember, we're here to locate Professor Lindfors and get him back to Britain. That's our prime objective, not starting a private war with the Germans."

G.I. Joe nodded in agreement. Then he clambered over the rocky area between them and the more level ground and, half crouching, vanished toward the township.

Action Man and Ernie Perkins began to take stock of their stores. The spare clothing in the packs was sodden and the packets of hard biscuits were wet through, too. Their eating appeared to be confined to the tins of bully beef each pack contained. The three pairs of ski-boots dripped water — only the skis themselves had suffered the immersion in the sea-water without harm. They had no weapons at all.

"Not much use," said Perkins, looking forlornly at the items spread out on the rocks.

"They'll dry out," replied Action Man optimistically. "And the Norwegians will help us. They don't like being occupied by the Germans, believe me."

There was nothing else they could do until G.I. Joe came back and they settled down, sheltering among the rocks, fighting the cold which was slowly claiming them.

*　　*　　*　　*　　*

"It's an old fish storage shed, or something like that. It stinks and it's dark but it'll do for us." G.I. Joe was back and helping the others to carry their possessions across the rocks. "And what's even better, it hasn't been used for ages."

"How'd you know that?"

"Dust and cobwebs. All over the place. Take my word, no one's been in that shed this winter."

The shed was tall and black with a covering of tar on the outside. Inside there were the staves of broken barrels and lengths of rotting rope lying about. There were dust-covered windows high in one wall through which a little light filtered; but it was a haven, warm and dry.

They opened two tins of bully beef and ate ravenously, scooping the meat out with their knives. Hungry as they were, none of them could stomach the salt-water-soaked biscuits. To slake their thirst they put handfuls of snow in the empty tins and waited until it melted.

"We'll light a fire as soon as it's dark enough," said Action Man. "Can't risk it yet. If someone sees smoke coming from a shed that's supposed to be unused, they'll come to investigate."

And they blessed the Northern latitude that

brought darkness so early for, by the time they considered it safe to light a fire, all three were shivering with the cold.

They lit their fire in an old bucket, filling it with the broken barrel staves and soon the sides of the bucket glowed red. Their clothing steamed as they dried it and they heated two more tins of bully beef. Within half an hour of the first flame flickering into life, they were warm and thinking of making their next move.

Action Man had a map. It was tattered and stained with sea-water but still decipherable. He stabbed a finger at it and said: "This is where we are." He moved his finger, tracing a line down the map. "This is the village where Lindfors is staying. It's not more than twenty kilometres. We can walk it."

"Let's pack up and get going, then. Is there a road? I mean, maybe we won't need these things after all." Ernie kicked at the skis lying on the floor. "We can use the road. Keep our eyes open; if we see a Jerry patrol, we can hide. It'll be quicker."

"The skis were only to use across country . . . if we'd landed where we should have. Here." Action Man pointed to the spot on the coast where their ship had sunk.

Ernie Perkins who was standing near the door with an eye to one of the many cracks in it, said: "Reckon there are many Jerries in these parts, Action Man?"

"There are bound to be some. Not many,

though. Probably just a small garrison but able to call on support from the big towns if they need it." Something about Perkins' intent preoccupation with the crack in the door made him add: "Why?"

The little man turned with a big grin on his face. "Because there's two Jerries walking straight toward us," he whispered. "Looks like a coupla blokes on patrol who are going to stop for a smoke."

They could hear the heavy jack-boots of the German soldiers now. Louder and louder. A shadow passed the door and then came a thud as though something heavy had been leaned against the shed wall.

"That's his gun," Ernie whispered.

Faintly they could hear the gutteral tones of the two Germans. Then the acrid smell of cigarette smoke drifted through the planking. Ernie Perkins grinned again and raised his thumb at the others. "Told you so."

"We could do with their weapons," whispered G.I. Joe, raising his eyebrows. "What say we grab 'em?" He unsheathed his Commando dagger. "Won't take long. No noise."

Action Man thought swiftly and then nodded approval. "We need their guns," he agreed. "Let's get 'em."

Action Man eased open the door and stepped softly outside, waiting until G.I. Joe made the long walk around the far end of the hut. They now had the two Germans trapped between them. Together they edged around the corners of the building.

The Germans, preoccupied with their cigarettes and staying out of sight, never knew what hit them. The long knives of G.I. Joe and Action Man found their targets and their victims dropped soundlessly. Within seconds, their bodies, guns and ammunition, were being hauled inside the shed.

"Sooner we go now, the better," said G.I. Joe. "These two guys will be missed as soon as they fail to check in. Maybe two hours from now . . . maybe ten minutes." He kicked the three packs and spare clothing they'd dried. "What about this stuff?"

"Leave it," said Action Man crisply. "We won't need it. We should be with the Professor soon. By midnight we'll be on our way back to England."

"How?" asked Ernie. "Our boat back got sunk, remember?"

"We'll take one. There are dozens of fishing boats in this harbour. We'll come back and get out that way. The Professor may even have friends who can help us . . . arrange for a boat to be waiting. Anyway, let's get moving. Now."

All they took with them, apart from the recently captured automatic weapons, were the white camouflage trousers and fur trimmed jackets in the packs.

"Help make us invisible if we have to take to

the snow," observed Action Man grimly. "Okay, out the door."

They had no need to go through the streets of the fishing port as the place where they expected to find Professor Lindfors lay to the south. Ten minutes after leaving the shed they were tramping along a narrow road. It was covered with snow, but the snow was packed hard and they made good time in the dim twilight.

* * * * *

Voorsgaard, the village where Lindfors was staying, was as silent and still as the grave. Action Man, G.I. Joe and Ernie Perkins, crouched among fir trees on a slope above the village, watched and waited.

They had been in position some ten minutes and so far had seen nothing more than two children in brightly coloured anoraks in the streets. No lights showed from the windows. The village seemed deserted.

"Which is the Prof's house?" asked Ernie.

"The one standing by itself to the east of the church." Action Man pointed into the gloom. "Can't miss it. No lights on there or movement."

"That doesn't mean there's trouble," said G.I. Joe. "Anyone with any sense will be indoors in this cold." He shivered. "We'd get inside, too, if we weren't barmy."

"Better to be safe than sorry," observed

Action Man. All the same he agreed with the American. There was little to be gained from further observation. The sooner they got down and met the Professor the better. He felt reasonably sure there were few if any Germans in the village.

They slipped like ghosts through the streets, passing the wooden-boarded houses, each one with a set of steps leading up to the front door. Wisps of smoke rising here and there from chimneys was the only sign of life.

The house near the church was just as silent. Action Man waved G.I. Joe to the cover of the low stone wall that surrounded the little church-yard and took up position himself by the end house.

"Go and find out what's going on, Ernie," he whispered. "If it looks like trouble, drop down on your face and me and G.I. Joe will open up. We'll fire half a dozen bursts and then stop for one minute. That's when you run back here. Okay?"

Ernie nodded acceptance of his role and drawing one deep breath stepped out into the street and moved quickly to the front door of the lone house. Without hesitation he rapped his knuckles on the front door.

Action Man raised his machine-pistol and sighted it on the door an inch above Ernie's head. From the corner of his eye he could see G.I. Joe taking similar aim.

Ten seconds passed . . . twenty. And then

the door opened a few inches. Action Man heard the low murmur of Ernie's voice on the cold air. The door opened wider and Ernie stepped inside. In the brief moment in which he was outlined against the light he turned and raised an arm, beckoning.

Action Man gestured for G.I. Joe to go forward and the American ran swiftly, machine-pistol held ready. He, too paused at the door and Action Man heard him call. "Okay, Action Man. This is the place."

Inside, a roaring log fire threw a cosy glow around a room which gleamed with polished woodwork. Two comfortable armchairs were drawn up close to the fire and on a small table were the remains of a meal for two people.

The man who had opened the door was an elderly Norwegian and his fearless brown eyes peered at them from above a straggly moustache.

"You would like something hot to eat and drink?" he said with true hospitality. "Sit down while my wife prepares a meal. It will not take long."

"We've come for Professor Lindfors," explained Action Man directly. "Where is he?" As he was talking he inclined his head, signalling G.I. Joe to go upstairs. He wanted to be sure they had not walked into a trap, although he felt this was unlikely.

The Norwegian allowed G.I. Joe to mount the stairs without question. "You have come too

51

late, my friends," he said. "Professor Lindfors is not here. He was taken away by the Germans yesterday morning."

"Taken away? Where?"

"To Castle Richbleau." The Norwegian shrugged. "It is further south, about one hundred kilometres. Not far from the town of Domahar."

"When will he be back?"

"He will not be back," the Norwegian replied heavily. "My wife and I were engaged to live here as the Professor's servants, you understand. To look after him while he worked." He gestured vaguely toward the rear of the house. "He had a laboratory out there where he conducted his experiments."

G.I. Joe came down the stairs and in response to Action Man's look of enquiry, shook his head. "It's clean," he said shortly.

"Why did they take him?" asked Action Man resuming his interrogation. "Did the Germans say?"

The Norwegian nodded. "I overheard them. They said he was in danger here. He would be safer in Castle Richbleau." He spread his hands. "The Professor did not want to go. He asked how he was to continue his work. But the Germans told him the castle had more facilities than he had here."

"Did they say what sort of danger he would be in if he stayed?"

The elderly man nodded again. "The Ger-

mans feared the Allies would try to kidnap
him." He smiled wanly. "They were not far
wrong, either, eh?"

"Not to kidnap him," grated Action Man.
"The Professor wanted to go to England. He
knew the Germans would use his experiments.
He wanted the Allies to have the results of his
work."

A woman came through from the back bearing a tray of steaming cups. She set them down
without a word and withdrew.

"Please . . . drink," said the man.

"First, how do we get to this castle place?
You said one hundred kilometres."

"You could go by road but you would never
arrive. It is patrolled regularly. There is a pass
through the mountains but that would mean
using skis. The pass is also patrolled but there
would be more chance."

"That's the way we'll go." Action Man sat
down in an armchair and raised a cup of steaming coffee. "Here's wishing us luck."

"I wish I could be of more help. But . . . I
wish you luck, too."

＊　　＊　　＊　　＊　　＊

At dawn's barely discernible light, the cold in
the mountains was bitingly cruel. The breath
from the three men ski-ing through the pass
froze in droplets on their fur-trimmed hoods.
Action Man led the way, breaking the snow and

the others followed in his tracks.

Not only had the Norwegian from the Professor's house supplied them with skis, he had found them light rucksacks and a supply of food, enough for their journey.

Another patriot in the village had given them a German rifle and ammunition together with half a dozen stick grenades. "We take them from the Germans and use them against them when we have the chance," he had told them. "You are welcome to them."

The worst part of their journey, they had been warned, would be the first three hours when it would be all uphill. After, they should make better time on the downhill slopes.

For some time, after their early-morning start, Action Man had secretly wondered if they would make it. But now they were high among the mountain peaks which before had seemed inaccessible.

At mid-day, a thin sun shone through the cloud and helped to warm them. They made camp under a gigantic overhang of rock and ate the food the Norwegians had prepared. It was a type of porridge, sweet and syrupy but it restored their energy amazingly.

"If it's downhill most of the way from here, I reckon we'll make it before midnight, if we keep going," said G.I. Joe. He looked at the others. "And I'm all for keeping going. I don't fancy spending a night out here."

"Nor me," seconded Ernie Perkins. "Stone

me, you go to sleep out here in this cold, and you might not wake up again."

"You reckon you can keep going that long?"

G.I. Joe and Ernie Perkins nodded their heads in agreement.

"Okay, then . . . we press on." Action Man rose to his feet and walked to where they'd stuck their skis and ski-poles upright in the soft snow. The sunshine, weak though it was, glinted and sparkled on the snow slopes that stretched endlessly before them. "We're going to look like currants on an iced cake out there," he told them. "If there's a Jerry patrol for fifty kilometres around, they'll see us. And they'll be on skis, too."

"They gotta catch us," grunted Ernie. "We can ski!"

G.I. Joe caught Action Man's eye and nodded. "It's a risk but like Ernie said, better than freezing to death at night."

Exactly one hour later as they skied quickly in great curving loops across a vast plain of snow, they saw four figures on the slopes high above. They too were ski-ing and approaching fast, curving left and then right, making to cut across their own line of progress.

"Jerries?" queried G.I. Joe.

"Too far off to tell," answered Action Man, his lips closing to a thin line. "But I don't think we should wait to find out."

They increased their speed, turning more down the long slope, shortening each leg of their turns. They could no longer avoid the hillocks and humps which were everywhere on the slope. Their speed brought them upon the obstacles before they had time to turn away. And more and more their ski-run became a series of air-borne leaps.

Ernie was the first to fall. He had taken the lead and instead of meeting a hump squarely, he hit the side and spun away, sliding on his back, his skis breaking free and sliding fast on the slippery surface.

"I'm okay," grunted the little man gamely, brushing the snow off his arms and legs. "Where's the darned skis?"

Action Man had gone in pursuit of the skis and he brought them back, moving slowly uphill, side-stepping.

"We've got Jerries after us, all right," he commented as Ernie stepped into the ski bindings again. "Make out their helmets. Rifles slung."

"Moving too fast to shoot," put in G.I. Joe staring at the four small figures on the snow above them. "But they're making time."

Ernie, Action Man and G.I. Joe thrust their ski-poles into the snow and moved on. Since the pursuit had first started they had come a long way and now for the first time since they'd left Voorsgaard they saw trees. Fir trees, still a long way below, maybe two miles, but the start of the tree-line. If the Germans were still behind and close by the time they reached the trees, the

shooting would start. And Action Man wanted to avoid shooting. He didn't want to take the risk of his tiny force being reduced.

And then another hazard presented itself. In their effort to out-ski the German patrol they had changed direction, moving more directly down the mountainside. Now they could see the darker outline of a chasm some four hundred yards ahead. It appeared to stretch in both directions as far as the eye could see . . . and it was at least fifty yards wide.

Ernie had seen it too. "We can't get over that." he yelled, leaning on the edges of his skis and coming to a violent and snow-swirling halt. The others pulled up beside him, panting.

Together they scanned the terrain. Then G.I. Joe pointed. "Over there. A snowbridge. We can cross there."

"Will it hold our weight?" Ernie looked anxiously at Action Man. "I've heard about these snow-bridges. It's just snow, nothing more. Some of 'em could carry a lorry . . . others are no more than a crust. You step on 'em and . . . that's it. You drop." He sighed heavily. "And those crevasses can be awful deep, mates. Miles!"

Action Man glanced back over his shoulder. The German patrol was scarcely more than three hundred metres behind and coming on at speed.

He gave Ernie a frosty smile. "Let's go and find out how strong this one is, Ernie . . . we've had it if we stop here."

They pushed off. Now less than two hundred metres separated them from the German patrol and they could plainly hear voices shouting at them.

Their skis hissed over the snow. Plumes of white powder rose behind them. The crevasse came closer and closer and they formed up in line ahead to cross the narrow snowbridge. Now, to Action Man's eyes it looked even more flimsy than it had from a distance.

G.I. Joe was leading, Ernie close behind. Action Man slowed his pace slightly, tugging at the two stick grenades he carried thrust into his belt.

G.I. Joe hit the front of the snowbridge and bounced into the air coming down squarely in the middle of the slender path. The crevasse on either side yawned deep and black. And then he was on the far side with the exultant cry of Ernie Perkins behind ringing in his ears.

"We did it!" yelled Ernie. "We're blooming well over!"

They had both slowed and Action Man came over at speed. He did not slow but went past them in a crouching weaving run. "Get moving." He yelled. "Grenades!"

Neither man had any idea what Action Man meant but they obeyed unhesitatingly. Then Action Man slid sideways in a bone-juddering stop. They came up beside him and turned to watch the German patrol.

The Germans came in a bunch. They'd seen the three Commandos ski safely over the bridge and their fear of its strength had vanished. They saw their quarry halted not far ahead and they closed in eagerly for the kill.

Action Man unslung the machine-pistol from his back and pulled back the cocking handle. G.I. Joe did the same and Ernie slid a cartridge into the breech of his rifle.

Then, as the Germans reached the centre of the snowbridge, it exploded with a great roar. Masses of snow laced with the flash of flame erupted, obscuring the ski-ing Germans from their sight.

When the upflung snow settled the Germans had disappeared . . . and the snowbridge no longer crossed the crevasse . . . it, too, had gone.

"Stone the crows!" Ernie stared incredulously at Action Man. "What happened?"

"Grenades," said Action Man laconically. "I pulled the string on two of 'em and dropped 'em on the snow-bridge as I came across. He turned his skis downhill. "Timed it just right."

They hit the tree-line five minutes later and their progress became much slower as they turned and twisted among the towering pines.

The speed they had achieved during the long run before the German patrol served a useful purpose by shortening the time it took them to reach Castle Richbleau. Even so, the moon had risen by the time they reached their destination.

They were still high up but they skied out of the trees to the top of a long smooth slope which dropped dramatically down to an enormous ice-covered lake. Half a mile away a long causeway jutted out to an island in the lake's centre and on the island, rising sheer from the water were the stone walls of Castle Richbleau. In the moonlight its castellated turrets and towers cast an eerie shadow across the ice beneath.

"That," said Action Man, "is where they've got Professor Lindfors."

"And we've got to get him out?" G.I. Joe's eyes roamed over the seemingly impregnable fortress.

"That's it," said Action Man. "We'd better start thinking about how we're gonna do it!"

CHAPTER THREE

IN..... AND OUT!

They sat among the trees and finished the rations they carried in their packs. Then they checked their weapons and spare ammunition.

While they ate, they had observed the Castle. It was a formidable task they had been set. The frozen lake surrounding the island was patrolled every half hour or so by groups of German soldiers riding motorcycles.

"Metal studs in their tyres," said G.I. Joe when they had first seen the motorcycles coming across the ice. "Gives 'em grip." He grinned back at the others. "Before the war they used to have 'speedway' on ice . . . same as you guys had your dirt-tracks in Britain."

Ernie Perkins looked gloomy. "If they come round all night, how are we going to get across? They'll see us. It'd take ten minutes to get across the ice at least. Then we've got to find a way in. They'd spot us."

Action Man was inclined to agree with Perkins. Yet the causeway was out of the question as an entrance. German sentries were

stationed at the castle end of the causeway and on the landward side there was an outpost built of concrete manned by more guards. He was quite sure there would also be sentries on the castle ramparts.

G.I. Joe sounded as gloomy as Ernie Perkins. "We could try shooting our way in, but I don't think we'd make it. Three of us . . . and who knows how many Germans? Could be three hundred in that place!"

A bone-chilling wind had risen and it moaned softly through the pine branches overhead; and with the wind came the first few flakes of snow. It settled upon their clothes and within minutes they were covered.

"If Jerry doesn't get us . . . this will." G.I. Joe swept his arm around in an all-embracing gesture. "Know what we will be by morning? Frozen meat!"

Castle Richbleau had all but vanished in the flurry of snowflakes. Action Man stood up and clapped his hands, shaking the snow from his body. "What we have to do," he murmured, "is hope that this weather gets worse!"

"Worse?" Ernie Perkins glanced at him in bewilderment. "What for?"

"Because, if this snow falls faster, no one is going to see us cross that lake."

Ernie Perkins looked down at the castle and his face split into a grin. "Hey, you're right. Never thought of that. It's better than a blooming smoke screen."

The snow did get worse. An hour later it was blowing a blizzard and the three adventurers ski-ed down the final slope to the lake confident they would not be seen.

So blinding did the snow become, all three of them bounced off the snow and on to the lake before they realised how close they were. Of the causeway and the castle there was no sign at all. Everything was hidden behind an impenetrable curtain of whirling snowflakes.

They buried their skis in the snow and bent their heads to the howling wind, setting off across the frozen lake. They kept a course slightly to their right knowing that if they missed the castle in the blizzard they must strike the causeway. In the event, their navigation was true. They were five paces from the castle wall before they saw it rearing solidly in front of them, its upper battlements hidden in the blizzard.

They each put a hand against the wall and began to follow it round.

"What are we looking for? A door? Open and inviting us in?" Ernie Perkins felt the bitter cold more than the other two and his patience had worn thin. "Why don't we face up to it? We can't get in. We've had it!"

"At the worst, there's always the front door," whispered Action Man soothingly. "But I'd rather get in without anyone knowing."

And then he found what he had hoped he would. A small window, no more than four feet above the ice level. It had three iron bars on the outside and the glass in the frame was coated on the inside with black paint. But it looked a possible means of entry.

Action Man and G.I. Joe immediately began work prising at the cement in which the bars were set, working with their long Commando knives. Once they had chipped out one piece of cement the rest came away easily, crumbling as they pushed the blades underneath, levering and twisting.

When the bars had been removed Action Man motioned to G.I. Joe to be ready with his machine-pistol. "I'll knock in the glass. It's covered in some black-out material. If there's anyone inside, they'll come to the window to find out what's up. Let 'em have it . . . and then we go in as fast as we can. We won't get another chance."

G.I. Joe nodded. He stood facing the window, gun at the ready, finger on the trigger. Action Man stepped quickly forward, smashed the hilt of his knife against the window panes and the glass fell inside with a noise that seemed to them to be like a giant alarm bell going off.

Nothing happened. Action Man beckoned Ernie Perkins forward. "Use your rifle on the rest."

The butt of the rifle knocked in the remainder of the glass sending it tinkling to the floor inside, trimming the frame clean. No one came to see what was happening. No voice sounded.

Action Man unslung his own machine-pistol and cocked it. He put one leg over the sill and went inside in a single sinuous movement. Almost immediately his face appeared. "Come on. No one about. It's some sort of cellar."

"By golly, it's good to be in out of that wind," muttered Ernie a few seconds later as they all stood in the darkness inside. "If I get some leave when we get back from this job . . . I'm going to spend the lot of it sitting in front of a fire, wearing a fur coat."

Action Man put out a hand, feeling for the wall. Then he moved slowly along until he found the handle of a door. It was unlocked and opened on oiled hinges as he pulled it towards him. Beyond he could see a dimly lit corridor, stone walls and a stone flagged floor. There was no sound. Their entrance had gone undetected.

Gently he closed the door again. G.I. Joe and Ernie were standing close at his back.

"There's no use rushing out there and trusting to luck that we find the Professor," he whispered. "This is a big place and he could be in one of a hundred different rooms. So this is what we do.

"We move out of here and find a German. Just one by himself. We bring him back here . . . without making a noise . . . and bring him back alive. Everyone here must know where the Professor is located . . . so we make our prisoner tell us. Then we go get him. Okay?"

G.I. Joe and Ernie nodded agreement. "Sounds the best plan. I can't think of anything else," said G.I. Joe. A smile flashed swiftly across his lips. "Let's hope the first Jerry we see . . . is a cissy who prefers to talk rather than . . ." He left the sentence unfinished but the others knew what he meant. They didn't want to torture a man, but they would if they had to.

Once again Action Man pushed open the cellar door. This time, gun at the ready, he moved out with the others following soundlessly.

The lower corridors of the castle were illuminated with burning brands held in iron baskets hanging against the walls and the flickering flames left dark pools of deep shadow between each brand. The Commandos flitted from one shadow to the other. They had left their white ski-ing outfits in the cellar and were no more than shadows themselves.

They came to a flight of steps that led to a landing and then turned and went higher. Here they suddenly found luxury. Electric bulbs gave light and the corridor before them, wider than before was carpeted in the centre with a broad strip of rush matting.

"What now?" G.I. Joe put his lips close to Action Man's ear to whisper as they hesitated, looking at the brilliantly lit expanse before them. "Do we still take a prisoner?" The American jerked a thumb back over his shoulder. "It's a heck of a long way now to drag someone who won't be all that keen to go."

Action Man had been thinking the same thing himself. "Change of plan," he said. "We'll just ask politely where the Prof is!"

"Politely?"

"With this?" Action Man patted the barrel of his gun. "If we don't get a fast answer . . . we'll ask someone else!"

G.I. Joe and Ernie understood. Action Man heard the metallic sound of G.I. Joe cocking his gun and the more definite click of the bolt of Ernie's rifle.

They stepped out into the corridor, feeling like actors in the spotlight. There was no way they could creep up on anyone without being seen.

And then, when they were in the centre of the long corridor, they heard someone walking toward them. Walking steadily, hard heels banging loudly even on the rush matting.

At the far end appeared a German officer, the rank tabs of Lieutenant on his collar. He was engrossed in a sheaf of papers he held in his hands, head bent, reading as he walked.

He was no more than three yards from the Commandos before he became aware of their presence. He looked up with a frown, taking one more step before he realised something was wrong. Very wrong.

Action Man, G.I. Joe and Ernie Perkins stood shoulder to shoulder completely blocking the corridor. Three gun barrels trained upon the German's heart.

"You speak English?" snapped Action Man.

The officer gaped, gulped twice and replied. "Ja . . . er, yes."

"Then it's your lucky day," said Action Man softly. "Or it will be if you answer our questions. If you don't, you'll die. Understand?"

The Lieutenant nodded wordlessly.

"Where can we find Professor Lindfors?"

A long pause and then: "Up the stairs. Second floor."

"He's lying!" G.I. Joe's voice was harsh. "Don't trust him."

The German was regaining confidence and composure. "If you don't know where the Professor is yourself . . . how do you know I am not telling the truth?"

"Turn around. Put your hands on your head." Action Man jerked the barrel of his gun menacingly. "Now! Do it now!"

The Nazi officer jerked into life. He turned, hands on head. The papers he'd been carrying fluttered to the ground.

"Move!"

The procession went forward slowly. "Wh-where to?" asked the German uncertainly. The confidence he had regained had left him again.

"Up the stairs," grated Action Man. "Second floor. We'll find out if you're lying or not!"

At the end of the corridor they entered a vast open area. Above was a huge domed ceiling with an enormous chandelier of more than fifty lights hanging by a chain. Below, a courtyard with huge double doors on the far side. Around the sides on their level ran a landing guarded by ornate railings. Here and there doors led off at intervals; they were all closed.

"That's the main gates out of here," said G.I. Joe peering over the guard railings at the double doors. "Worth remembering."

"You . . . the stairs to the second floor." Action Man prodded his prisoner with his gun muzzle. "Keep moving."

They circled half of the landing before turning into a narrow opening where a short flight of steps rose upwards. The German with his hands still on his head mounted ahead of them.

"Hold it!" Action Man pressed the muzzle of his gun in the officer's back.

Below, in the courtyard, three armed German infantry men marched stolidly across the area and vanished from their sight without looking up.

Action Man nodded at the German who turned and continued up the stairs. At the top they came out into another corridor. The German turned left and they followed until he halted before a door.

"Professor Lindfors' room?"

"Ja . . . yes."

"Go inside. Walk into the centre of the room.

Don't turn round and don't take your hands off your head."

G.I. Joe put a hand out to touch Action Man's arm. "If this is the Prof's room, shouldn't there be a guard on the door? I mean, he's being held prisoner here."

Action Man raised the muzzle of his machine-pistol until it pointed at the officer's head, just behind his ear. "Well? You heard what he said. Why no guard?"

"It is not necessary." There was no doubt the man was telling the truth. He was sweating with fear, his eyes flickering from the gun barrel at his head to Action Man's grim face. "No one can escape from here. No one can leave the castle without crossing the causeway and there are guards there at both ends."

"Okay, go in!"

The door was unlocked and opened easily. The German obeyed his instruction and walked forward into the centre of the room. The light through the opened door lit him up, a perfect target.

No sound came from inside and Action Man gestured to his friends. "Inside."

They went in like the well-trained team they were. G.I. Joe stepped past the door and took up position with his back against the wall, machine-pistol moving slowly from side to side covering the entire room. Action Man went straight across to the far side and dropped to one knee. Ernie Perkins closed the door behind and stood with his back against it.

"Light!" snapped Action Man.

Ernie Perkins had already found the switch and he depressed it, flooding the room with light.

It was a large room with wooden panelling on the walls. Large, but sparsely furnished with a chest of drawers, a wardrobe and a bed. In the bed, sitting up, staring in amazement was a middle-aged man with a short spade beard, neatly trimmed.

"Who is he, Joe?" demanded Action Man. "Know him?"

"No doubt about it!" G.I. Joe was grinning hugely. He walked to the bed his hand extended. "Hi, Prof. Remember me? Joe? In your chemistry class in the States. I was the goofy kid who could never get the Bunsen burner to light."

Professor Lindfors sat up straighter. "Yes, I remember you, Joe." His English was hesitant but clear. He turned to include Action Man and Ernie Perkins in his astonishment. "But . . . what are you doing here? Who are these men? Why . . . ?"

"We're here to take you home, back to England, sir," put in Action Man. "We'd have had you back sooner only the Germans must have got wind of our plans and whisked you away from Voorsgaard."

"How many of there are you?" the Professor could still hardly believe what he was hearing.

"Have the Allies taken Castle Richbleau?"

"Well, that's a matter of opinion." G.I. Joe crossed to the wardrobe and took out trousers and a thick sweater, tossing them on to the bed. "We think we've taken the Castle . . . but the Germans don't know about it yet. Except him." He jerked his thumb at the still sweating officer.

"There's just the three of us. We'd rather like to get away as soon as we can, sir." Action Man was smiling but his voice carried a chill note of command. "Get dressed as quickly as you can. Put something warm on, we may have to do some cross-country work and it's cold outside."

The Professor swung his pyjama-clad legs out of bed. "Yes, yes, of course. I will not be a minute. There are papers I must take, too. Papers relating to my work, you understand?" He pointed at the chest of drawers. "You will find them in there and a briefcase in the bottom of the wardrobe. Please put all the papers in the case. All of them."

Action Man nodded to Ernie Perkins and the little man leaned his rifle against the wall and finding the briefcase, began filling it. By the time the case was full, the Professor was dressed; over all he pulled a fur coat. "As you say, Action Man, it is cold outside."

"What do we do with him?" Ernie stood by the German officer. He had his rifle back in his hands now. "Lay him out? Shoot him?"

"Tie him up. Use the bedclothes . . . and gag him. We don't want him hollering his head off."

The German was swiftly trussed up tighter than a chicken ready for the oven. He lay on the floor glaring at them.

"Have you plans? For . . . for getting out?" The Professor moved with the three men as they stepped out into the corridor. "You know the only way to leave is across the causeway?"

"We came in through a window . . . from across the lake. It's frozen." G.I. Joe whispered in the Professor's ear. "We'll go out the same way. There's a blizzard blowing. No one will see us."

But that exit was barred to them.

They arrived back in the cellar without anyone in the castle seeing them. But when they went to the shattered window they came to a sudden halt.

Outside, not ten feet away, were three German motorcyclists. One was on foot and he had in his hand the iron bars which they had prised from the window. He was showing them to his comrades and an excited discussion was taking place. And it had stopped snowing. From the window they could see across the lake as far as the shadowy tree-line where they had waited earlier.

"That's torn it." G.I. Joe glanced down at his wristwatch. "Seven-o-clock. Not all that dark any more, either."

"And getting lighter," said Ernie Perkins glumly. "I'll tell you this much for

nothing . . . we ain't got a chance of getting across that lake. Those blokes out there know someone's broken in . . . they're going to blow the gaff any minute."

The interior of the cellar was now visible in the half-light from the window. It contained a huge pile of neatly rolled rush mats similar to those they had walked upon in the lower corridor.

"Pick up those mats and follow me." Action Man went to the door and through it. "Hurry."

They did as they were told, the Professor helping. Action Man led them to the end of the corridor just before the entrance to the circular electrically-lit landing. He reached up and took one of the burning brands from its bracket on the wall.

"Pile the mats up. Get another torch. We're starting a fire."

"A fire?" The Professor stared at Action Man in wonder. "Why on earth should we do that? You'll only bring the Germans down on us."

"And the fire brigade, I hope," answered Action Man cryptically. "Now come on, lads, get cracking. Set those rush mats on fire."

Leaving G.I. Joe and Ernie Perkins to carry out his orders, Action Man went down the corridor to the circular landing. At the far end he raised the matting and deliberately held the burning brand against it. Flame leaped along the matting; smoke rose billowing to the ceiling. Action Man came back down the corridor touching the brand to the matting here and there. Within seconds the corridor was aglow with flame and acrid smoke.

Now G.I. Joe lit the bundles of rush matting they had brought up from the cellar. They had a pile which thickly covered the corridor floor. It burnedrfiercely, forcing them to retreat.

"Get more of the stuff from the cellar. I want a fire here that's going to keep going for an hour or so!"

By the time they had carried everything that would burn from the cellar and dumped it on the fire, bells were ringing throughout the castle.

"How many fire appliances do they have in the castle?" Action Man asked the Professor as they retreated into the cellar and shut the door behind them. "Can they cope with what we've started?"

"I'm sure they can't. There are only a few hoses and hand extinguishers. They'll telephone Domahar and ask for help."

"That's what I thought." Action Man seemed satisfied.

"We'll be cooked if we stay here," Ernie Perkins pointed to the door where wisps of smoke were already finding their way underneath. "Look at that lot."

"We wait until the fire brigade arrives," said Action Man. "Then we get out that window and move round to the main gates. Every German in the place will be concentrating on that fire.

They won't be bothering about us. For one thing, they don't know we're here. Those motor-cycle men won't get much of a hearing when they try to report a broken window. Everyone will be too busy."

"So? What do we do then?" Even G.I. Joe was baffled.

"We pinch the fire engine," said Action Man simply. "They'll drive through the main gates and into that courtyard we saw. We go in, board the engine and drive out. The guards on the landward end of the causeway won't stop us. Why should they? They'll think the firemen are coming out."

G.I. Joe looked at Action Man admiringly. "I'll be durned if that ain't one of the craziest ideas I've ever heard. And it could work."

"It's got to work, otherwise we're stuck here," responded Action Man grimly.

"What if we meet Nazi soldiers in the court-yard, when we're nicking the fire engine?" asked Ernie Perkins.

"You'll know what to do." Action Man tapped his machine-pistol: "It's us or them, Ernie."

The Professor had been standing by the broken window and now he turned and spoke. "If you had asked my opinion before, I should have said your plan had almost no chance of succeeding."

"But now?"

"Now, I think it might." A slight smile

crossed the Professor's face. He indicated the window. "If you care to look out, you'll see the fire engine from Domahar. It's just turning onto the causeway."

Ernie Perkins broke into a cheer which turned suddenly into a fit of coughing as a gush of smoke swirled around him from beneath the door. "Let's get out of here, then. I'm getting kippered."

Their exit through the window went unhindered. A thick layer of snow on top of the ice-bound lake deadened their footsteps as they ran around the outer wall of the castle.

There was no one at the castle end of the causeway and the huge double doors were wide open. From within they could hear shouts of command and feet running across the stone flags.

"They're busy, all right," grinned G.I. Joe.

"Let's get up and make sure," murmured Action Man. "See what kind of opposition's waiting for us."

The top of the causeway was some ten feet above their heads but Ernie Perkins made a back and Action Man and G.I. Joe clambered on top of him and hauled themselves up. They stepped quickly to the doors and peered cautiously inside. There were men there but no one was watching the doors.

"You next, Prof," said Action Man. He helped the scientist up to the road and Ernie followed. "As soon as we go through those gates, Prof," the big Commando instructed, "you make for the fire engine. Don't look to see what's happening anywhere else. We'll take care of that. You get into the fire engine cab and sit tight and sit as low as you can. On the floor if possible. There may be bullets flying. And when we move . . . we're going to move fast. Got it?"

Professor Lindfors licked his lips and nodded. "You are brave men, bold men," he commented. "I am learning to trust you."

"Then let's go."

Action Man, G.I. Joe and Ernie Perkins ran in through the double doors with the Professor behind. There was a fireman in uniform at the back of the fire engine attending to four hose connections. Hoses wriggled in long lines from the rear of the engine and rose in the air, draped over the guard rails of the landing above. Smoke billowed in clouds from the corridor where the fire had been lit and more firemen were up there, playing jets into the corridor. Three armed sentries, their rifles slung, were standing beyond the engine staring upwards.

At the sound of running footsteps on the stone flags behind them they turned. Their mouths fell open.

"Englanders!" yelled one, more quick-witted than the others. "Englanders!"

Action Man and G.I. Joe opened fire simultaneously—withering blasts from the machine-pistols that dropped the Germans where they stood.

An officer appeared above on the landing. His eyes took in the scene below and he started to pull a revolver from its holster. Ernie Perkins fired once and the officer sagged, fell against the railings and very slowly toppled over, hitting the ground with a thud.

The Professor was already in the fire-engine driving cab. G.I. Joe and Ernie Perkins climbed in after him and Action Man ran round the front of the vehicle to the driver's side. As he did so, the fireman who had been at the rear came towards him.

Action Man raised his machine-pistol. "Norwegian?" he called? Ashen-faced, the fireman nodded. Action Man lowered his gun. "When they come to, tell 'em the Commandos were here," he grinned. "And tell 'em we'll be back again one day . . . to free all Norway!"

"Free all Norway?" the fireman repeated. It was obvious he did not understand. But Action Man's smile had its effect. The fireman smiled, too. "English!" he cried. "Good luck."

Action Man slid in behind the wheel, crashed the engine into gear and the giant machine jerked forward, gathered speed and charged out onto the causeway. Behind, the hose connections were pulled apart and water gushed across the courtyard, swirling around the four bodies lying there.

G.I. Joe was sitting replacing the magazine of his machine-pistol. He found it difficult under the bumping and bounding of the racing fire-engine.

Action Man at the wheel had his eyes glued to the far end of the causeway where he could see the concrete emplacement and four armed guards standing beside it.

"Press that!" he pointed at a large red button on the dashboard.

G.I. Joe did as he was told and an automatic bell began clanging with ear-splitting force somewhere behind their heads.

"Don't shoot," shouted Action Man. "Not until they do."

But there was no need for shooting. As the huge red vehicle crashed over the far end of the causeway and turned on to the main road, the four German guards stood aside. One of them waved a hand.

"We've blooming well done it!" yelled Ernie in delight. "Did you see that German. The idiot waved at us!"

"We're out of the Castle," admitted Action Man soberly. "But we've got a long way to go before we're out of Norway!"

CHAPTER FOUR

EVERYTHING HAPPENS!

As the fire engine thundered along the road that skirted the ice-bound lake, Action Man reached up and turned the switch that silenced the clamour of the automatic bell. Away to their left, the castle stood in gaunt splendour. From somewhere in the centre of the turrets and towers a dark spreading stain of smoke arose, climbing high on the cold air.

"Looks like it's still going nicely," murmured G.I. Joe.

"Reckon they realise the Prof's missing yet?" Ernie Perkins was staring ahead at the snow-covered surface of the road as it rushed towards them. "They're going to send out a few signals when they do."

"They'll be spreading the word now anyway. They've got four guys shot back there . . . and someone's pinched their fire engine!" G.I. Joe, shook his head. "Whichever way you look at it, they're not going to like it."

Action Man looked at Professor Lindfors and asked: "How far to Domahar? I don't want to go charging through a big town on a stolen fire engine."

The Professor seemed quite undisturbed by the situation in which he found himself. He was as calm as though he were lecturing students in college. "This road leads directly to Domahar. It's about fifteen kilometres further on."

"Any turn-off roads?"

The Professor nodded; "Several. Where are you heading for?"

"The coast. Our arrangements with the Navy have gone wrong . . . but we'll get away. We'll take a fishing boat or something like that."

"You just can't take any boat you see lying around." The Professor sounded brisk and businesslike "You want to sail it to England, I presume, with the four of us aboard. For that, my friend, you'll need all sorts of things. The journey may take two or three days, according to the weather. You'll need fuel for the boat's engine. You'll need food for four people. Suitable clothing. Navigation charts. Sailing a boat is not as simple as you would think."

G.I. Joe caught Action Man's eye and winked. "I used to put up with this for four hours a week when I was a kid at college," he grinned. "The Prof sure knows how to talk."

"Okay, so we're going to need stores and things," Action Man agreed. He swung the wheel of the fire-engine hard over, narrowly avoiding a small, grey saloon car which came at them from the opposite direction. "How do we go about getting 'em?" In the driving mirror he watched the grey saloon swerve from side to side in their wake and then settle on a steady course again, finally disappearing around the far bend. The driver had been a civilian; he probably thought he was lucky not to have been hit by the engine.

"We go back to the village where I have been living," said Lindfors. "There I know many people. People I can trust. People who will help me . . . and you. We go to Voorsgaard. You turn right about four hundred metres further on."

"We can't go all the way in this!" G.I. Joe banged the dashboard in front of him. "I mean, a fire engine isn't the most inconspicuous vehicle you can think of! We'll have to change transport."

Ernie Perkins reached for his rifle and operated the bolt, pumping a bullet into the firing chamber. He grunted one word: "Trouble!"

They had just rounded a bend, sliding slightly on skidding wheels, and ahead of them the road stretched out long and straight.

Away in the distance, about three hundred metres, was a road block. Oil drums had been placed in line down the length of the road, diagonally, starting on one side and moving across so they directed all oncoming traffic towards a covered truck parked on the verge. There a German soldier stood holding a machine-pistol. In the back of the truck two other soldiers sat behind a Spandau machine-gun. An officer stood straddle-legged in the centre of the road. He looked very menacing.

"Are they past the turn-off road?" snapped Action Man. He had neither slowed their speed nor increased it.

"About two hundred metres this side. We've got to pass them before we can head for Voorsgaard."

The officer was still in the middle of the road and he was now waving both arms above his head, an obvious indication for them to stop.

"If they knew who we were," observed G.I. Joe slowly, "he wouldn't be standing out there like that. The castle have probably only reported the theft of a fire engine."

"And the dead men we left behind," said Ernie Perkins.

"Maybe, maybe not," said G.I. Joe. "But if someone had told me there was a fire-engine thief on the run who was trigger-happy, I wouldn't stand in the middle of the road and wave at him!"

Action Man took his foot off the accelerator and allowed the vehicle to slow. "We don't want to start any long range shooting," he said. "If we do, that Spandau will rip us to pieces before we can get at it. I'll coast in, making it look as though we're going to stop. When I give the word, everyone open up with everything we've got and I'll step on the gas!"

Action Man pushed his machine-pistol over to the Professor. "You know how to use this?"

Lindfors picked up the weapon, looking intently at it as though making up his mind about something. Then he smiled wanly at Action Man . . . and pulled back the cocking handle. "I am a scientist, not a soldier," he murmured, "and yet it seems fighting is the only way left to us."

"You're durned right, Prof!" G.I. Joe was holding his gun below the level of the windshield, his finger crooked around the trigger-guard. "I tell you this much, and it's a scientific fact . . . if we don't gun these guys down . . . they'll gun US down! I know what my choice is gonna be."

They had reached the diagonal line of barrels and were moving slowly towards the officer who shouted arrogantly: "Stop and get out with your hands over your heads. You are from Castle Richbleau, ja?"

"Ernie," said Action Man quietly. "Shoot the guy with the Spandau. The rest of you take the officer and the other two men. NOW!"

Ernie Perkins's rifle cracked like a whiplash and the machine-gunner in the back of the truck dropped sideways. The startled face of his companion stared at them with round eyes for a split second before Action Man stamped his foot down on the accelerator.

The fire engine surged forward with the full power of its twelve cylinders. The officer leaped to one side and G.I. Joe, leaning from the window fired a long burst at the other soldier.

They were more than a hundred metres down the road before the second man on the Spandau pulled it from beneath the body of his comrade and brought it to bear.

Bullets zipped into the road beside them, spouting the snow in a dozen mushrooms of flying ice. Bullets rattled loudly as they struck the rear of the engine and ricocheted away with a snarling whine.

Action Man spun the wheel and slid the giant vehicle into the turn-off road, tyres screaming. Another burst from the Spandau but this time the bullets flew high and wide; and then they were hidden from view by trees and rising ground.

"Now we're really going to be for it, lads," Action Man said, turning to his companions with a broad grin. "When Jerry hears what just happened, he's going to alert every garrison in Norway. They'll shoot first and ask questions afterwards. The hand-waving is over!"

Half an hour later, they ran out of petrol. The engine coughed once, twice, and then died. Action Man brought the vehicle to a halt, running it off the road and into the trees.

They had not passed a house since they had broken through the road block. Around them, snow hung from the drooping branches of the fir trees and a mist swirled close to the ground. The air was brittle with cold and silence enclosed them in their own small world.

"We walk." Action Man swung down to the ground. "We walk until we find somewhere to shelter for the night. Then we carry on walking."

No one disagreed with him. There was nothing else to do.

But as time went by, they all realised how vulnerable their position was. At any moment a German motorised patrol might come along the road and yet, they dare not leave the road for the cover of the forest. Under the trees the snow was deep and treacherous and without skis they would make no headway at all.

"How far before we reach a house, Prof?" asked G.I. Joe.

Lindfors shrugged. "I'm not sure. There may be a farmhouse along here somewhere, I don't know. But there is not a village before Voorsgaard."

"How far's that?"

Again the shrug of the shoulders. "I'm not sure. Say, thirty five kilometres?"

Ernie Perkins moved his rifle from his left shoulder to his right. "Unless we find transport, I reckon we've had it," he grunted.

"Car coming!"

As they had already decided, they immediately split into two groups, each pair running off the road to left and right. Taking cover in the trees they turned and faced the road, guns at the ready.

The car that came into view was old and sagging badly on broken springs. It moved slowly and at the wheel they could see a German soldier sitting hunched deeply into his overcoat.

Professor Lindfors was hiding behind a tree with Action Man and the British Commando tapped him urgently on the shoulder. "Get out there and wave him down, Prof," he said. "You'll be okay in your civilian outfit. He won't suspect anything." He tapped the barrel of the machine-pistol. "If he does, we'll attend to him."

The Professor obeyed at once, stepping from the trees on to the road just before the old car drew level. He waved both hands at the driver, shouting for him to stop.

"What is it?" the German braked his car to a standstill and wound down his window.

"I'm in trouble. My car has gone off the road," said the Professor, inventing his story on the spur of the moment. He waved his arm back at the trees from which he had emerged. "The brakes failed. Can you give me a lift, please?"

"I'm only going as far as the railway bridge," the driver replied. "But you can come with me. I'll drive you back to Domahar afterwards. A signal light is broken there," he explained. "I have to repair it. It will not take more than a few minutes."

Action Man had made a detour round the car and now he came up behind it. He pushed the Professor to one side and thrust the muzzle of his machine-pistol against the side of the German's head. "Open the door and get out." he commanded icily.

The German's mouth dropped in astonishment and his face turned a bilious green.

"Out," snapped Action Man. "I have no time to waste."

The man recovered his wits and moved so quickly in his attempt to obey, he opened the door and fell out on to the road. He rose to his knees, his hands in the air. "Don't shoot." He squawked. "Please, don't shoot."

Action Man ignored him and peered into the car. On the back seat was a bag of tools, otherwise it was empty. "I won't shoot you. All I want is your car."

G.I. Joe and Ernie Perkins joined them. "He's got to have a gun somewhere," said Ernie.

"In the boot, sir," said the German, anxious to please. "My rifle. I'm a railwayman," he added. "I was a railwayman in Hamburg before I was called into the Army. I-I'm not a very good soldier."

"You're telling me," sniffed G.I. Joe. "Okay, buddy, you're on foot from now on."

"Car coming!" Ernie Perkins yelled the words desperately. All four of them had been so concerned with their capture, they had failed to hear the sound of an approaching engine. Now it was almost upon them, no more than fifty metres away, still hidden from view around a bend. Then it appeared. A German Army truck.

The driver saw them at the same time as they saw him. But this was a patrol. A patrol which had been sent out with the specific purpose of searching for them.

The truck slid sideways off the road as the driver applied the brakes. Hardly had it come to a halt when the canvas flap at the back was brushed aside and German soldiers began to spill out and run for cover in the trees.

Action Man, G.I. Joe, Ernie Perkins and the Professor dropped behind the car. An automatic weapon began firing and bullets smacked into the side of the car. The German driver gave a yelp of fear and began to run down the road. Bullets cut up the hard-packed snow at his feet before he fell and lay still, an ominous stain spreading beside him on the white snow.

"Prof, you and Ernie run when I say so. Make for the trees behind us," snapped Action Man. "Me and G.I. Joe will give you covering fire. Move as soon as we open up."

G.I. Joe nodded and then he and Action Man stood up, firing over the car's bonnet into the dark shadows of the trees on the far side.

"Keep firing. Count five . . . and then we run after the others," shouted Action Man. "There's too many of 'em . . . we've got to disappear fast."

Their fire pinned down the German soldiers. On the count of five, both men turned and plunged into the forest, stumbling, almost falling in the deep snow.

They could see Professor Lindfors and Ernie Perkins ahead of them weaving through the close-packed trees. Behind, the German soldiers waited, making sure no one had been left at the car.

G.I. Joe and Action Man caught up with the others. They were all gasping for breath in the cold air.

"Where to?" gulped Ernie.

"Just keep going. Until we lose these guys behind . . . or find a place where we can make a stand." Recovering his wind, Action Man's eyes darted around. The ground ahead rose steeply and he pointed. "Up there," he said. "We'll make it to the top before they get here. When they try to follow, we can pick 'em off as they come up."

"What if they just keep us cornered until they bring up reinforcements?" Professor Lindfors' voice was weak. "We cannot keep running for ever."

"We'll think about that when we get up there," Action Man moved to the slope and began to climb. "Hurry. Move it."

Halfway up the slope they all stopped, startled. Behind them sounded a tremendous explosion and a brilliant flash of light spread through the fir forest.

"The car!" said G.I. Joe. "They've blown it up. Now they know we're not still there, they'll be after us." He nodded back in the direction of the way they had come. "They won't have much difficulty there."

They all looked back. Winding through the trees was the jumbled snow of their footprints, a trail easily visible.

Action Man resumed the climb and the others followed. At the top they halted in astonishment. As far as they could see, in both directions ran a single-line railway track. The hill they had been climbing was a railway embankment. To their left, the track rose steeply, climbing to the not so distant mountains.

"The soldier in the car said he was a railwayman," recalled Ernie Perkins. "This is where he was headed. Poor guy . . . nearly got there, too."

"Let's get moving. We can make good time along this track."

"Maybe we can catch a train?" Ernie Perkins grinned cheekily. "Reckon there's one due?"

"If one does come along, and it's going that way," said G.I. Joe, gesturing toward the gradient. "It'll have to slow down for the hill. That's steep. We could get aboard with a bit of luck."

From the fir forest they could hear twigs breaking and shouts as the German soldiers began to make their way in pursuit.

"Train or no train, we can't hang around waiting." Action Man stepped on to the wooden sleepers and adjusting his pace to the intervals between the sleepers, began to run. It was a lot easier than struggling through the snow in the forest.

And then, when they were halfway along the steep gradient, and reduced almost to walking pace, they heard the shrill whistle of a train.

"Going our way, too," said G.I. Joe, stopping and looking back. "And here come the lads," he added, as he saw German soldiers reach the top of the embankment and step out onto the line. "They're sure to spot us."

There was almost three hundred metres between the Germans and their quarry now, but there was nowhere Action Man and his friends could go. Once off the railway track they would again become bogged down in the deep snow. They had to follow the rails until something happened; until they found some sort of shelter where they could fight off their pursuers . . . or until they dropped. It was a grim choice.

The gradient was now so steep they moved at a snail's pace. And the Germans, still on the relatively flat section, moved twice as fast, gaining with every step. Action Man privately decided the Germans would open fire when they had reduced the gap to about two hundred metres. He knew he must be ready for that moment and his head constantly turned, keeping the Germans in view.

So it was Action Man who first saw the train behind them. It was over a mile away and belching smoke from the engine. Behind the engine came a long line of goods trucks. It was moving quite swiftly and its whistle sounded again, shrilly, urgently.

"We'll hop aboard," hissed Action Man in a sigh of relief. "This is our salvation, chaps."

"We'll not get aboard if it goes past at that speed," Ernie Perkins looked at Action Man in consternation. "Stone me, chum . . . we'll do the job for the Germans . . . kill ourselves."

"It won't be going that fast. Not up this hill."

"What if the Germans have the same idea . . . and hop on, too?"

"I don't think they will. For one thing, they're further down the hill than we are. It will be going too fast for them. For another thing . . . how do they know we won't bunk off into the trees as soon as they get aboard? They could lose us that way. My guess is they let the train pass . . . and if we try to get aboard, open fire and hope to pick us off."

"Won't the driver stop if he hears shooting . . . and sees us climbing on his wagons?"

Professor Lindfors joined in the discussion. "Not if the driver is a Norwegian," he declared firmly. "He will be on your side."

"Then that's what we do. Try to jump aboard the first wagon after the engine's passed. That way the other wagons will shield us from the German fire." He raised his eyebrows at the Professor. "Think you can manage it, sir?"

Lindfors nodded. "If I'm in difficulty, I'm

sure I can rely upon the rest of you to give me a hand." He smiled broadly. "After all, I am the reason you came to Norway. I'm sure you won't leave me behind if you can help it."

By now the train was level with the German soldiers who had moved off the track to allow it to pass. They were about two hundred metres behind Action Man's group.

The train whistle shrieked again. It was slowing down very fast as it hit the steepest part of the gradient. Smoke belched from its funnel in dense black clouds and to Action Man's delight, he noticed how the wind blew it back into the faces of the Germans:

They're not going to find it easy shooting, he thought. Not through a smoke screen!

Now the engine drew level. It was travelling at the speed at which an average man could run along the flat. They had a brief glimpse of the fireman, face blackened with soot, staring down at them, and then the first goods wagon drew level.

They all missed that one but G.I. Joe leaped at the second and found a handhold on a rope which zig-zagged along the side, hooked into staples, a rope that held down a tarpaulin covering the truck's contents.

Ernie Perkins jumped for the same one G.I. Joe went for. The little man clung on one-handed, lost his rifle, lost his legs and was dragged along, yelling for help. But Ernie had to help himself, Action Man was too busy helping Professor Lindfors.

The Professor was surprisingly agile. He and Action Man jumped at the third truck, found their handholds among the ropes, and clung on. Action Man hauled himself up on muscles that were like steel springs. Then, turning, he grabbed Lindfors by the wrists and slowly but surely hauled him to safety. A rifle cracked and a bullet parted the air an inch above Action Man's head.

Ernie Perkins, legs flailing, had at last managed to get both hands to the ropes and he too hauled himself atop the wagon, panting, exhausted.

"Don't get up, pal," grinned G.I. Joe, lying beside Ernie. "Jerry's letting go with everything he's got. I don't think he likes what we've done."

The air was filled with flying lead. Splinters suddenly flew off a corner of the truck as a bullet struck home. But the train was drawing steadily further and further away and finally the shooting stopped.

"We made it, buddy." G.I. Joe rose to his knees and glanced back. The German soldiers, standing on the line were growing smaller and smaller in the distance. On the next truck back, Action Man and the Professor were lying face down. G.I. Joe looked down at Ernie and gave the little man's shoulder a jubilant punch. "We've done it. We've given 'em the slip."

"I'm cold!" snorted Ernie petulantly. "It's

blooming freezing up here."

Action Man leaped the intervening space between the two trucks and turned to help Professor Lindfors across. All four crouched, swaying to the lurching of the train over the metals.

The train driver had seen them board his train and they became aware of a hand waving at them from the driving cab.

"He's calling us to go up front," said G.I. Joe. "What do you reckon?"

"He is a Norwegian. He will not do you harm," said Professor Lindfors. "And it will be warmer there," he added. The hands and faces of them all were blue with the cold.

"Then let's go." Ernie Perkins stood up and without waiting for approval, leaped on to the coal bunker ahead. Watching, Action Man saw the fireman in the cab turn to help Ernie down until he stood beside him. "Come on," yelled Ernie. "These guys are okay".

When they were all in the cab, huddled before the roaring flames that could be seen flickering at the open hatch of the firebox, the driver said: "You are English?"

"We'll get off before we reach a station," said Action Man. "You'll slow down for us?"

The driver nodded but before Action Man could speak again, he said: "You know what we are carrying?" He could tell by the look on Action Man's face that the answer was 'no', so he supplied the information himself, in one word. "Munitions!"

"For the German troops," added the fireman. He spat deliberately over the side. "We have to do this work . . . or the Boche shoot us."

Professor Lindfors who had been listening intently said quietly: "You wouldn't be upset if we . . . er . . . got rid of your load then?"

The driver's face lit up with a great smile, the smoke blackened features splitting wide. "Now, if you should do that, the Boche would not be very pleased," he said. "Even if it brought the defeat of the Germans just one day nearer, it would be a good thing, yes?"

"It sure would, pal," agreed G.I. Joe.

The train was in the mountains now and still going uphill. "How far is it to a station?" asked Action Man.

"From here, eight kilometres." The train driver glanced ahead. "A small place where we stop to take on water after the climb."

"We'll stop just before we get there," said Action Man quietly. "You two can walk on . . . and leave the rest to us." He clapped the driver and the fireman on the shoulder. "You can tell the Germans we forced you off the train at gunpoint."

*　　*　　*　　*　　*

The train halted four hundred metres from the mountain top and the fireman and driver, with a farewell salute, walked on. Neither of them looked back. There was a long walk ahead of them.

Action Man stood in the cab and watched them go, then he ordered his companions down on to the track. "I'm going to blow up this little lot," he grinned at G.I. Joe. "Like the driver said . . . it won't do Jerry any good at all. There's a lot of ammo on this thing."

"We'll want fuses. It's gonna take time," G.I. Joe looked around anxiously.

Action Man smiled broadly. "It won't take long," he said "Watch!" He pushed the long handle of the brake forward, releasing the restraint on the wheels. Slowly the train began to roll backward down the gradient. It gathered speed, faster, faster.

Action Man jumped off when he was sure the train was not going to stop.

"Great balls of fire!" exclaimed the American in awe. "Boy, I get the idea now!"

Together they all stood watching the train recede. It gathered pace rapidly, moving away, downhill. It began to shake from side to side with its own speed. Faster. Faster.

A mile away down the track there was a gentle curve. The first truck held to the rails, taking the bend. And the second. But the third truck jumped the rails. The train seemed to bulge sideways. The third truck took the trucks following with it and the weight pulled the two trucks that had already passed the curve off the

rails.

For a second the trucks ran on upright beside the track before turning over and sliding, breaking up, splintering.

Then came the engine. It too was pulled off the track by the coupling connecting it to the overturned wagons. It hit the first over-turned wagon, leaped into the air and came down sideways with a crash they could hear.

The boiler split and steam spurted high into the air. Redhot coals spewed out in all directions. Some of it settled upon the smashed ammunition trucks.

The first explosion was quite small. Perhaps a box of machine-gun bullets exploding. Then another and another and suddenly fire spread so swiftly the eye could scarcely follow.

Like an enveloping blanket the wrecked trucks became covered with a flat pool of flame. For a full second nothing happened and then, from the centre of the flames rose a huge black cloud. Higher and higher in uncanny silence the column towered. Flame laced the black column, searing white-hot particles began to shoot out in all directions, trailing plumes of white smoke.

The shock wave hit Action Man and his companions like a blow in the stomach, sending them staggering against each other. And as they staggered, the noise of the explosion came to them.

A noise so deafening it beat them to the ground. A roar of sound that battered their eardrums and rolled around the mountains in deafening echoes of terror.

When they picked themselves up they were silent, awestruck by the thing they had witnessed.

"Let's go," said Action Man quietly. "We'll follow the track away . . . until we're forced off it."

They followed him wordlessly. There was nothing to be said.

CHAPTER FIVE

THE WAY OUT!

At the watering halt on the mountain top, the driver and his fireman greeted them with delighted smiles. With them were two elderly men who manned the small halt.

"Many times have I wanted to do that," cried the driver in delight. He made a descriptive action with one hand. "Boomm! Just like that. Finish to the whole lot."

"You won't be held to blame?" said Action Man.

"Blame? Us?" the driver sounded astonished. "How could we be to blame? Back there a dozen German soldiers saw you board my train. They knew you were desperate and armed. How could I, an unarmed train driver, stop you from doing what you wanted to? No, my friend. The Germans will not blame us. Beside, railwaymen are very short in Norway, the Germans want us to work for them. They will not harm us."

"I thought that's how it would be." Action Man held out his hand and shook with the driver and fireman. "You are good men. Norway must be proud of you."

One of the older men stepped forward. He looked worried and anxious. "You will not get away, friends," he said. "Not unless you leave the railway line and go through the mountains." He pointed to the telegraph poles that ran parallel with the tracks. "The men who were chasing you are not fools . . . and they are well equipped. Already they will have tapped the wire and made a signal to the town. It is easy to do." He looked along the track as though expecting Germans to appear already. "They will send out a train from that way . . . to meet you, so they will think. You will be cut off unless you go that way." He turned and looked at the towering peaks. "That way."

"We need skis to go into the mountains." G.I. Joe looked glum. "And we don't have skis."

"You can ski?" The old man's voice was high with surprise. Then an expression of joy came over his face. "Then we have solved your problem. You can ski!"

He trotted back to the cabin where the watering crew lived and returned a moment later carrying two pairs of skis. "There are two more pairs in there," he cried jubilantly.

"Do you know the way through the mountains . . . to Voorsgaard?" asked Professor Lindfors as they all equipped themselves with the skis. "I have never been this way before."

"Just follow the line of that peak there." The driver gripped Action Man's shoulder and standing close to him pointed his arm straight at a distant peak. "Always keep that peak ahead of you and you will reach Voorsgaard," he declared. "Look at it . . . fix it in your mind. See how it curves on this side . . . like the face of a man with a bald head, yes?"

There was a faint resemblance to the man's description and Action Man nodded. "Okay, we'll go that way."

The old man stepped forward again. In his hand he held a coil of thin rope. "Take this, a length each." He began to cut the rope into long lengths. "Tie it to your belt at the back. Then, if there is an accident you will find each other."

"An accident?"

"Avalanche," said the old man. "That big bang you make. It will have loosened the snow. It is possible that another bang . . . a small one even . . . or a shout . . . may start an avalanche." He turned to the others for support. "Is that not so?"

The fireman and driver nodded sombrely. "He's right, there's a big danger of avalanches."

"How will this help us?" asked Action Man holding up the length of cord that was tied to the back of his belt.

The old man said: "If the avalanche comes and you are swept away . . . you will be buried . . . but not the cord. The end will show above the surface, just a small part, perhaps, but enough for someone to find . . . and then they find you, too."

"Sounds a great idea." Ernie Perkins looked back at the long length of rope dangling behind him. "I'm for it."

They shook hands all round, wished each other luck, and then the three soldiers and the professor set out, gliding in long running strides over the level ground and then starting to traverse as they reached the downhill slopes.

Action Man raised his eyes and saw the peak ahead. It now looked very much like a bald-headed man and he knew he would not get the peak confused with any other.

*   *   *   *   *

They were weaving their way down a deep valley, patterning the virgin snow behind them with intertwining trails from their skis when they heard a strange noise. A fluttering banging noise which came from above.

Over the shoulder of a mountain slope, not very high, came a strangely cumbersome machine, camouflaged with white and black markings and bearing the Iron-cross of Germany on its fuselage. A helicopter.

There was no way of avoiding being seen. They were on a slope that stretched for hundreds of metres in all directions. From above, they must have stood out like four flies on a table cloth.

It passed overhead so low they could see the lone occupant at the controls inside.

"He can't fly that thing and shoot at us," said Ernie Perkins in relief.

"He'll radio back. Tell his pals he's found us," said G.I. Joe. "He'll have the wolf packs out after us in no time."

The pilot of the helicopter made no attempt to attack. He hovered some way off, circling.

"Keep going," grunted Action Man. "It'll be dark soon. We'll lose him."

The slope they were on became steeper and their speed increased. Action Man kept his eyes on the bald-headed man peak ahead and judged they had little more than ten kilometres to go. And the darkness was increasing as the Arctic day drew in. The helicopter overhead was almost invisible.

"Hey, he's heading for home." G.I. Joe made a sliding halt that flung up snow in a great spray, and pointed a ski pole in the air. "He's given up."

They could just make out the helicopter. It was flying towards one of the peaks that towered high above them.

Ernie Perkins laughed: "If he doesn't go a bit higher, he's going to bash into the top. He's far too low."

But, sixteen metres or so from the top of the mountain, the helicopter pilot banked his machine and began to retrace his path, flying close to the rocky wall.

And then Professor Lindfors realised what was happening. "He's trying to start an avalanche!" he shouted in horror. "He'll do it, too . . . the noise that machine makes could easily start the snow moving!"

They stood in a group, staring up at the mountain top, fascinated. The helicopter made another pass across the rocky face before rising suddenly, almost vertically.

"He—he's done it!" Professor Lindfors' voice was a whisper.

"Done what? I can't see anything?" Ernie Perkins, too, spoke in a whisper.

"There. Look, now. Do you see it? That . . . cloud. It looks like a cloud . . . moving . . . this way . . . down the slope!" The Professor staring upward with the others, touched Action Man's arm. "You'll hear it too, . . . booming . . . rumbling, getting louder."

"Hey, the ground's shaking!" Ernie Perkins stared at the others in horror. "He's right, it's an avalanche."

"Get out of here!" Action Man turned on his skis and started off downhill. "We'll race it!"

I don't think you'll do that, my friend, thought Professor Lindfors. An avalanche will travel at over one hundred and sixty kilometres an hour. All the same, he turned and moved after the three figures who were already skimming fast over the snow below him. There was nothing else to be done.

The moving snow, its front edge six metres high and being pushed along at incredible speed by the thousands of tons of snow moving behind, hit them after they'd moved no more than one hundred metres.

"Kick off your skis!" yelled Lindfors as he felt the on-rush of air that preceded the snow wall. "Get them off." And then he fell and was buried.

The other three went under immediately after. For a moment an arm here, a leg there, showed above the tumbling snow and then disappeared. The snow rushed on to the valley bottom and piled high up the further slope.

The noise stopped. The helicopter returned and flew low over the barren slopes. Satisfied, it rose and soared above the peaks. Finally the noise of its vanes vanished, too.

G.I. Joe who had ski-ed years before in America, had turned to face the avalanche as it hit him. Some dimly remembered instruction he'd received as a boy on the ski slopes at home, came to his mind. As he was engulfed he struck out like a swimmer, swimming against a strong tide. When he could swim no more, he put his arms across his face and allowed himself to go with the snow. It was exactly what a mountain guide in the Canadian Rockies had taught him, when he'd been a little more than ten years old . . . and it saved G.I. Joe's life and the lives of all his companions.

When G.I. Joe came round after being

knocked unconscious, his arms were across his face and they formed a pocket of air in the snow around him. He scrambled about with his hands, enlarging the pocket until he could move his arms freely. Then he began to tunnel upward through the snow that covered him. He was lucky. There was no more than three metres of snow above his head. There could have been twenty metres and quite likely he'd never have dug himself clear. But he did.

The first thing he found was the Professor's briefcase Ernie Perkins had carried.

Then he set out to find his comrades and he blessed the old man who had told them to wear the trailing rope. The rope was yellow and he found some of it showing ten metres further down the slope. It was not the end of the rope, but the middle. Both ends were buried. G.I. Joe pulled the rope until one end came free, then he pulled at the other end, tracing it back through the snow until he knew he stood above one of his buried companions.

It was Ernie Perkins, alive and unharmed and conscious. G.I. Joe dug him free in little more than a minute and they began searching for Action Man and the Professor.

Without the ropes there would have been no chance. But the ropes were there; and they were found; just small portions showing in the snow but they led to the man beneath.

It was useless trying to find their skis, they could have been swept hundreds of metres further.

Action Man gave G.I. Joe a crooked grin. "Now we walk again," he said determinedly.

"Let's hope Jerry's given up then," said Ernie Perkins. "I mean, no skis, no guns, nothing. And we ain't gonna run far in this." He lifted a foot, which was an effort, for he was standing knee-deep in snow.

"We can do it," said Professor Lindfors. "There is not far to go. I have been in this valley before. I know the way from here. But it will not be easy."

*   *   *   *   *

Voorsgaard was in sight when Ernie Perkins fell on an ice-covered rock and broke his arm. They improvised a sling for the broken limb and although the little man's face was very pale and drawn with pain he made no murmur of complaint.

It was very dark and early morning when they finally reached the streets of the little village. G.I. Joe walked, supporting Ernie Perkins, who had suddenly appeared much weaker than anyone had thought. He stumbled continuously and would have fallen several times but for G.I. Joe's vigilance.

The Professor went forward alone to the house where he had been living before the Germans had forced him to move to Castle Richbleau. Watching from the shadows, Action

Man bit his lip anxiously as the Professor knocked again and again on the door without receiving an answer. Then, just as they were about to give up and try elsewhere, a light showed in the front room and seconds later the door opened a few centimetres.

"It's me, Professor Lindfors! Come, wake up, Olaf, surely you haven't forgotten me already?"

The old manservant's eyes lit up in astonishment and pleasure. "Professor! Professor . . . you have come back! Wonderful!" He opened the door wider and stepped aside. "Please come in, sir. I will make you a hot drink, food! Please, come in!"

"I have friends with me," returned the Professor, putting his finger to his lips and keeping his voice to a whisper. "English friends. I believe you met them earlier. Prepare us a meal, Olaf. Wake Helga and tell her what is happening . . . and that no word of our arrival must leak out. You understand?"

Olaf nodded once and turned into the house, disappearing along the hall in search of his wife. Lindfors beckoned to Action Man and the others and within seconds they were all safely inside.

Olaf prepared a meal and Helga, after one look at Ernie Perkins, insisted upon taking charge of the exhausted soldier. "He must go to bed at once," she declared stoutly, glaring at Action Man as though he alone were responsible for Ernie's condition. "Poor man. He needs care and attention."

When Olaf's meal was before them the Professor said: "I want you to go along to Ole Bjornson in the morning, Olaf. Tell him we must have a boat. One big enough to take four people across the North Sea . . . during winter weather . . . to England. It must be a fast boat, too. We will want stores for two, three, days and fuel."

"Ole will make the necessary arrangements," nodded Olaf without hesitation. In explanation, he smiled at Action Man and added; "Ole Bjornson is a fisherman. He has arranged the escape of many Norwegians in the past. Trust him."

"Tell him one more thing, Olaf. Tell him we want the boat by tomorrow night."

Olaf sighed and shrugged his shoulders. "I will tell him but it may not be possible, these things take time."

"The Germans think we were buried under an avalanche," said Action Man grimly. "But they will search for our bodies . . . they will want to be sure we were killed. When they don't find us there is only one place where they will come. Here!"

"That is true," agreed Lindfors. "They know I was with these soldiers, Olaf."

"Then you must rest," Olaf said resignedly. "Leave everything to me."

*   *   *   *   *

The four men slept like logs. Even the fear of a surprise visit from the Germans could not keep the weary men awake. When Olaf came upstairs and shook Action Man by the arm, it was five-o-clock the following afternoon. The big Commando had been 'out' for fourteen hours.

He came awake instantly. "You have a boat for us, Olaf? Is it arranged?"

"The boat is waiting, Ole Bjornson says you must all be in Klaagstad in one hour's time. I will take you there in my car."

"That's the fishing port where we landed in the rubber dinghy," nodded Action Man. "Okay! I'll wake the others." He added. "I hope Ernie's going to be fit?"

Ernie Perkins was far from fit. As well as his broken arm he had frost-bitten toes on his right foot. Helga had treated them as well as she could but she frowned disapprovingly when Action Man told Ernie what they were going to do.

"It is not good for him to travel," she declared. "He should be in a hospital."

"I'll be okay, love." Ernie patted Helga on the shoulder. "Thanks for looking after me. After the war, I'll come back and see you."

Helga smiled. "That will be nice, Ernie. Olaf and I will welcome all of you when it is peace in the world again."

Ernie looked very miserable and Action Man wondered why.

"It's because I lost that briefcase with the Prof's papers in," replied the little man. "No one's said anything about it until now. But it disappeared under the snow in that avalanche."

"The bag disappeared, Ernie, that's all," said G.I. Joe. He put his hand inside his battle-dress blouse and pulled out a great sheaf of papers. "I've got half of it, and Action Man's got the rest."

Ernie stared at the papers with popping eyes. "But how? I mean, I had charge of that bag. How'd you get the papers?"

"I was first to dig myself out of the avalanche," explained G.I. Joe. "First thing I saw was the bag. I thought I'd better take the papers out and scatter 'em, so's the Germans wouldn't get 'em if we were caught. Then I started to look for the strings . . . and found the rest of you. To tell you the truth, I forgot about the papers, too, after that. But I had 'em all the time, tucked in my battle-dress blouse." He chuckled. "They kept me quite warm!"

Action Man showed Ernie another batch of documents. "He gave me half last night just before we came to bed. We were going to set fire to 'em if the Germans barged in suddenly. With half each, we had two chances of destroying 'em. We reckoned half wouldn't be any use to Jerry if only one of us managed to do the trick." He patted Ernie on the back. "We should have mentioned it to you, Ernie, but we've all been a bit busy."

Ernie still thought he had failed somehow, but he managed a smile. "Well, as long as they're safe, I suppose it doesn't matter."

Professor Lindfors looked in the door, his face taut with urgency. "Please, we must leave. We must not be late at Klaagstad. Ole Bjornson will be waiting."

Klaagstad was still and quiet when they drove into the outskirts. Ole Bjornson met them at a street corner and as soon as they alighted from the car, Ole led them through a maze of alleys towards the waterfront. Olaf wished them a brief goodbye and turned the car round, driving back to Voorsgaard.

"We have one chance of success with this boat I have arranged for you," breathed Ole as they all crouched behind a pile of barrels that smelled overpoweringly of fish. "You do not give me enough time to find a Norwegian boat . . . so I get you a German boat."

"German?" Action Man and G.I. Joe repeated the word together, anxiously. "What kind of German boat?"

"It is what they call an E-Boat," whispered Ole. "Like you call in England an M.T.B., yes?"

"Great green-eyed snakes!" ejaculated G.I. Joe. "That's a warship. You're pinching a German warship?"

Ole grinned mischievously. "It is only a small one. You see, it will be easy. There is only one guard. I will come aboard with you to start the

engines. Then . . . zoom! You leave. Very fast.
It will be a big surprise and you will be well out
to sea before the Germans can make a chase
after you."

Action Man didn't like the idea of stealing a
German ship. It sounded risky. Unnecessarily
so, as his prime objective was to get the
professor back. "Why does it have to be an
E-boat, Ole?"

The Norwegian spread his hands. "A question of time. You want to get out of Norway
tonight. A German boat is the only boat which
will be fuelled, have stores, travel fast . . . and
be ready now. If you want a Norwegian boat, it
will take three days to get all this ready."

"Let's take the E-boat," grunted G.I. Joe.
"The sooner we're outa here the better."

Action Man nodded. "Okay," he said. "Show
us what to do, Ole."

The Norwegian led them further along the
quay, keeping to the shadows of the buildings.
A single electric light, shaded to cast a very
small light, hung by a wire over a small inner
dock. Inside the dock, rocking gently at their
moorings, were three E-boats. On a huge
bollard sat a German soldier, huddled in a
greatcoat, rifle slung across his back, hands
thrust deeply into his pockets. On the cold air,
his breath rose in misty patches as though he
were puffing on a cigar.

"The boat crews live over there." Ole
gestured to a large wooden house at the far end

of the street. "One boat is always kept on stand-by, ready for emergency. All we have to do, is knock out the sentry. Go aboard, and . . ."

"I know," interrupted Action Man. "And . . . zoom! We're away!"

Ole himself disposed of the sentry, creeping up behind him and knocking him unconscious with an iron bar.

"They're no good, not from a heavy blow," he said contemptuously, kicking the man's fallen helmet over the side into the water.

The E-boat was already facing seawards. Ole waited until everyone was aboard. Ernie Perkins, pale and exhausted was taken below where he rested on a bunk.

"You start the engines, so!" Ole pointed a stubby finger at a large red button on the control panel at the front end of the bridge where he crouched with Action Man. He indicated two levers. "These are the gears and speed throttles. Forward . . . and you go forward. Back . . . and you reverse. Simple, eh?"

"Seems simple," agreed Action Man.

"There is a gun forward and twin guns aft! Wait until I reach the shadows of the house . . . then start the engines and go." He offered his hand. "Good luck, my friend. Give my regards to Winston Churchill if you should see him."

"I'll remember," laughed Action Man. Then

he watched and waited until Ole was in the shadows of the houses ashore.

The engines started with a noise that echoed around the fjord like a thunderclap. A thousand sea-birds rose from their night-time rest, screaming in protest, circling angrily overhead.

G.I. Joe, standing at the twin after guns showed his teeth in a huge grin and gave Action Man the thumbs up sign. "Now you've woken every German in Norway, man . . . let's get outa here!"

Gears engaged and the E-boat moved forward. Action Man pushed the throttle lever forward and the stern of the vessel seemed to dig itself deep into the sea. The bows came up, water began to race past in huge foaming humps on either side and the neat houses on the quay dwindled into dolls' houses as the boat raced away.

Action Man shoved the throttle lever forward to its fullest extent and speed increased still further. Spray began to sting his face as it raced backwards over the glass coaming around the bridge.

Wow, thought Action Man, this is some boat. No one's going to give us ten minutes' start and then catch us! He hurriedly turned the spokes of the steering wheel as the enormous black rocky wall of the fjord rose out of the darkness ahead. With luck at this speed we'll be off the coast of Scotland tomorrow night!

*   *   *   *   *

Some time during the following night they neared the British coast then. The weather had worsened all day long and Action Man had had to take all the speed off the boat to prevent it from dashing itself to pieces against the giant waves that were building up. The wind, now at gale force, screamed through the rigging and the sea broke over the boat continuously. Lindfors and G.I. Joe had come up on the bridge with Action Man and together they strained their eyes, searching for land which they knew to be near.

"Where do you think we are?" asked G.I. Joe. "I mean, where do we land? We can't just steam into a port, the British'll think it's a German invasion and blow us to bits!"

"We can't use the rafts to get ashore, either," pointed out Lindfors. "Ernie Perkins is in a bad way. He'll not make it in a raft."

"I'll beach it," stated Action Man matter-of-factly. "Show me a sandy beach somewhere and I'll run this thing full tilt up the beach. We'll step ashore."

Lindfors clutched Action Man's arm. "Listen!"

They could all hear it then. The crashing, booming sound of waves dashing against a rocky coastline.

"Doesn't sound much like a nice sandy beach," muttered G.I. Joe. He pointed ahead. "Look there . . . you can see it. It's rocks. Big rocks . . . and breakers! You'd better ease off, man, or we're going to arrive there before we're ready."

The wave-battered rocks which a moment before had only just been visible were now quite plain to see. Every movement of the waves was pushing the E-boat nearer to them. Action Man swung the wheel and pushed the throttles forward.

"We're in some sort of current," he said grimly. "Wind and tide and a current . . . we're being swept ashore whether we like it or not." He gunned the engines again but the sideways movement continued. "Get Ernie up on deck," Action Man commanded crisply. "And see he has a lifebelt on. That goes for all of you."

All four of them stood on the bridge watching the black fangs of the rocks drawing closer. White water rose high, flinging itself forward before bursting with a tremendous roar on the rocks.

"Hang on, everyone." Action Man had seen a small gap between the jagged rocks. A gap maybe just large enough for the E-boat to pass through. Desperately he swung the wheel. There wasn't much time left now. Every wave was throwing them forward to their doom.

Slowly the bows came round. The gap seemed to move sideways to meet them. They were immediately above it. High above, perched on top of a huge breaker. Crossing his fingers, Action Man slammed both throttle levers full

forward. The answering roar from the engines could scarcely be heard above the clamour of the wind and waves.

But the E-boat responded. It seemed to hurl itself forward, still sitting on top of the giant wave. Through the gap and down, down into a swirling maelstrom of spinning white water.

The stern dropped sickeningly and all four were flung to the deck. The bows came round in a great arc. Water fell upon them in bone-shaking masses. Water that filled their mouths and ears and noses, choking, blinding.

But the E-boat still had forward movement. It thundered onward. Rocks grated under the hull and down below water started to spurt through a thousand cracks that appeared in the side. Then, with a shuddering crash, the German boat hit something solid and immovable.

It lurched back and tilted over at an impossible angle. Water crashed down upon the men on the deck and swept them off into the sea.

"Ernie!" yelled Action Man. He saw the little man, eyes wide, surge past him on a huge swell. Then G.I. Joe was beside him and they both lunged forward and grabbed Ernie Perkins.

Together, holding Ernie's head up, they fought their way forward. The waves lifted them and took them in a great rushing sweep, dropping them in a thunderous, roaring, creaming surf. They felt the ground beneath their feet. The backwash of the wave tried to pull them down, but they fought it. Staggering on, pulling Ernie with them.

A figure reared in front of them. It seemed huge. Then Lindfors yelled: "Okay, I've got him." And he pulled Ernie from their grasp.

Moments later all four of them sank exhausted to the stony shingle, clear of the sea. Water ran from their clothes, their faces, their hair. But they were safe.

*   *   *   *   *

The Professor's papers had suffered. Some pages were made indecipherable by the sea-water, but the majority of the scientist's work was there, intact.

In a barrack room in Portsmouth, the Professor stood with Colonel Cartwright and smiled at Action Man and G.I. Joe. He held out his hand. "I can never thank you two enough." He tapped the pile of papers which were on the desk. "When I sort this lot out I think the Allied cause will find much that will be helpful."

"Sorry it got so wet, sir," answered Action Man, "but we had a pretty wet landing."

"How is Ernie Perkins?" The Professor turned to the Colonel. "You will send him my good wishes?"

"Of course, Professor. Perkins is in hospital, resting. He's got one arm in a sling and needs a stick for walking, but he's making progress."

"I am asked to tell you something," said Lindfors, a twinkle in his eye. "The man from Intelligence, Mr. Blandment, has put in a special request for you two."

"Not another Special Assignment?" Action Man and G.I. Joe looked at each other blankly. "Not already?"

"He asked me to tell you there would be another special assignment very soon . . . but, in the meantime, with Colonel Cartwright's permission, you are assigned to fourteen days' leave."

Outside, Action Man looked at G.I. Joe and said: "Know where I'm going first?"

G.I. Joe nodded, grinning. "Same place as me, I shouldn't wonder. To the hospital to see Ernie."

THE END